AVENGER

Andy McNab
and Robert Rigby

GALAXY

PLUS

First published in Great Britain
by Doubleday, an imprint of
Random House Children's Books 2008
This Large Print edition published by
BBC Audiobooks
by arrangement with
Random House Children's Books 2008

ISBN: 978 1405 663007

British Library Cataloguing in Publication Data available

YLP

Printed and bound in Great Britain by
CPI Antony Rowe, Chippenham, Wiltshire

AVENGER

They bring death and destruction in their wake: influenced by their mysterious leader, known only as Black Star, vulnerable teenagers strap high explosives to their chests and blow themselves up. Maximum impact. Maximum destruction. London. America. Japan. Where will the Angels of Death strike next? Can they be stopped?

Despite the fierce objections of his grandfather, ex-SAS explosives expert Fergus Watts, Danny and his friend Elena are sucked into an undercover operation to find and destroy Black Star. As the trail leads to New York, the master of trickery and deception draws the teenagers into spiralling danger...

GLOSSARY

ACA	*Alias cover address.*
Brush contact	*Covert operation in which material or information is exchanged.*
Contact	*In a fire fight with the enemy.*
CTR	*Close target recce.*
DLB	*Dead Letter Box.*
ECHELON	*The code name of the British Security Services' electronic listening satellite.*
End ex	*End exercise, but also used to end a mission or operation.*
ERV	*Emergency rendezvous.*
FARC	*Colombian drug traffickers.*
The Firm	*The Secret Intelligence Service, MI6.*
FOB	*Forward operating base.*
GSW	*Gunshot wound.*
HE	*High explosives.*
IED	*Improvised explosive device.*
Int	*Intelligence.*
K	*Deniable operator.*
LS	*Landing strip.*

LUP	*Lay-up point.*
Mag	*A weapons magazine that holds the rounds.*
Make ready a weapon	*To put a round (bullet) in the chamber, ready to be fired.*
MoD	*Ministry of Defence.*
MOE	*Method of entry.*
MoU	*Memorandum of Understanding – agreement between governments.*
NVGs	*Night viewing goggles.*
On stag	*On guard.*
OP	*Observation post.*
PE	*Plastic explosive.*
'Pinged'	*When someone is first seen.*
Recce	*Reconnaissance.*
The Regiment	*What SAS soldiers call the SAS.*
RV	*Rendezvous (meeting place).*
Sit rep	*Situation report.*
SOP	*Standard operating procedure.*
SSU	*Special security unit.*
Stand to	*Get ready to be attacked.*
VDM	*Visual distinguishing mark.*

SURVEILLANCE TALK

Complete	*Inside any location —a car, building, etc.*
Foxtrot	*Walking.*
Held	*Stopped but intending to move on—i.e. at traffic lights.*
Mobile	*Driving.*
Net	*The radio frequency the team talk on.*
Roger	*OK or understood.*
Stand By! Stand By!	*Informs the team something is happening.*
Static	*Stopped.*
The trigger	*Informs the team that the target is on the move.*

HACKING TALK

Spoofing	*Hiding a computer's IP address.*
Root access	*When the hacker has control of the system under attack.*
Script	*A program written by a hacker.*
Script kiddie	*Novice hacker.*
Exploits	*Hackers' targets.*

CLASSIFIED – SECRET

SIT REP

Operation Black Star
Aim: Covert elimination, at whatever cost, of bomb master 'Black Star', known to be recruiting teenage suicide bombers via the Internet.
NB: Black Star's objectives unknown. No demands have yet been made, and the bombers appear to have no political affiliation.
Real name of target: Unknown.
Location: Unknown.

Special circumstances surrounding operation: Elena Omolodon (see below) recruited to assist in Operation Black Star with Danny Watts (see below) and Fergus Watts (see below).

FERGUS WATTS

AGE: 53
HEIGHT: Five feet, eleven inches
PHYSICAL DESCRIPTION: Hair—grey; eyes—blue; build—lean, wiry; distinguishing physical marks—noticeable limp due to bullet wound in right thigh
BACKGROUND: Infantry. SAS, Warrant Officer, special skills—explosives. Tours of duty include—Northern Ireland (decorated), first Gulf conflict (decorated), Colombia. Recruited as a Deniable Operator ('K') to infiltrate FARC, Colombia. Cover story—traitor, 'gone over' to rebels for money.

1

Watts's cover was deliberately blown by GEORGE FINCHAM (former head of the Firm's security section—now deceased). Watts wounded and captured after gun battle with Colombian anti-narcotics police. Imprisoned by Colombian authorities. Subsequently led mass jail break. Returned to Britain, route and date unknown. Traced through grandson, Danny. Captured but escaped from safe house with help from grandson and Elena Omolodon. Watts and grandson on run in Spain for six months, then encouraged to return to UK to assist in exposing Fincham as traitor. Fincham killed during firefight at culmination of Operation Payback. Watts severely wounded and now in recovery at ACA, Oxford.

DANNY WATTS

AGE: 17
HEIGHT: Five feet, ten inches
PHYSICAL DESCRIPTION: Hair—brown; eyes—blue; build—slim; distinguishing physical marks—none known
BACKGROUND: Orphaned at six, parents died in car crash. Various foster families until moved to Foxcroft, south London, residential home for teenagers, where he met Elena Omolodon. Applied for army officer training bursary. Rejected. Had never met grandfather but fed 'traitor' story and located (method unknown). Assisted in escape of Fergus Watts from safe house before going to Spain. Returned to UK with grandfather

and received superficial wounds in Operation Payback firefight. Now undergoing further covert operations training at ACA in preparation for possible second phase of Operation Black Star.

ELENA OMOLODON

AGE: 16
HEIGHT: Five feet, five inches
PHYSICAL DESCRIPTION: Hair—black; eyes—brown; build—slim; distinguishing physical marks—none known
BACKGROUND: Mother (Nigerian) deceased, father (Joey Omolodon, Nigerian) terminated during Operation Payback. Befriended Danny Watts at Foxcroft residential home. Assisted in initial escape of Fergus Watts from safe house and subsequent actions. Received superficial wounds in Operation Payback firefight. Now under 24-hour surveillance at ACA as lead contact for Black Star, whose help she sought on the Deep Web during Operation Payback.

Important: Omolodon unaware of father's termination. Imperative this situation remains unchanged if Operation Black Star is not to be jeopardized.

PROGRESS: TO BE UPDATED DAILY

Day 29

Psychiatric evaluation (see attached report from Dr Ruth Jacobson) indicates Omolodon's current stress levels rising as Black Star's grooming process becomes more intense. We continue to monitor the situation. Currently believe any risk to either the girl's health or the operation to be overstated.

Brush contact training continues badly. Danny Watts is generally enthusiastic but remains headstrong and unpredictable and a potential liability to the operation.

Fergus Watts's loyalties and the extent of his knowledge remain a matter of major concern. He suspects the Firm's involvement in Joey Omolodon's disappearance and I believe continues to operate to his own agenda.

IMPORTANT

There is no change to my conviction that all three individuals remain a threat to national security and will be expendable when Operation Black Star is concluded. Plans for their elimination should therefore be put in place at the earliest opportunity.

M. Deveraux

M. Deveraux

1

Charles Samuel Pointer III, Charlie Three to his friends, Chuck to his doting dad, was going to get a job.

His father would be impressed. Even though Charlie Three didn't need the work he was setting up for the Christmas vacation, he knew full well that his dad, Charles Samuel Pointer II, admired initiative and determination above all other qualities. Ever since the pioneering days back at the start of the twentieth century, the Pointers had been demonstrating their initiative and determination.

Charlie's great-great-great-grandfather had shown the initiative to emigrate with his wife and two children from Eastern Europe to the United States of America. And like thousands of other immigrants, Josef Podowski arrived at Ellis Island, in the shadow of the Statue of Liberty, with nothing more than the clothes he stood up in and the determination to succeed in his new life.

And he did. He was a grafter and he was clever. Even way back then, Josef saw that the future was in communications, and so he made it his business to get in there, starting at the bottom and working his way up.

A couple of generations on, with a lot of hard work, plenty of that famous initiative and determination, and a change of name from Podowski to Pointer, and the family fortune was well on the way to being made.

Charlie Three's grandfather, the great Charles

Samuel Pointer I, chose the new family name. He reckoned it sounded substantial and solid, pioneering yet well established and, most importantly, *American*.

The business continued to thrive and grow, and on the morning that Charlie Three left for his job interview, it was established as one of the nation's top computer and Internet research and development organizations, firmly placed at the cutting edge of the industry.

Some day Charlie Three was going to take over that business. But there was a Pointer tradition: no one got an easy ride; everyone had to get out there and show what they were made of by demonstrating that famous initiative and determination.

Charlie knew that maybe he wasn't quite as brilliant as his father, and certainly not as dazzling as the great CSP One, as he was known in the family. But Charlie was a trier, and as the only child, it was up to him to carry on the great Pointer tradition. There was no way he was going to let the old man down.

He had kept the interview a secret from everyone, even his father. The job was nothing special; a post boy, a gofer, working for an international finance company over the busy holiday period.

But Charlie Three knew that would impress his dad even more; he could already hear the old man's words when he told him he had the job. 'That's my boy. Get in there at the bottom, Chuck, and show 'em what us Pointers are made of.'

Charlie Three was up early. He dressed smartly and was feeling good as he stepped out into a bright morning and walked away from the family's East 96th Street penthouse apartment, which overlooked Central Park. He took the subway downtown towards Wall Street and the financial district, went through the security barriers into the building, and then joined the lines of workers drinking Starbucks and reading papers as they waited for one of the elevators to take them up to their offices.

On the way up to his floor he took a few deep breaths and repeated the old family maxim to himself: 'Initiative and determination. Initiative and determination.'

The elevator came to a standstill and Charlie Three stepped out onto his floor. He walked along the corridor and went through glass doors into the finance company reception area.

The long reception desk was close to one of the picture windows overlooking the city and the Hudson river and, beyond that, New Jersey. A young woman was standing behind the desk, staring out through the window. As he approached, Charlie Three saw the look of confusion and horror on the woman's face.

He followed her gaze out through the window and at the same moment heard the roaring noise. He recognized the plane instantly; he was interested in aeroplanes. It was an American Airlines Boeing 767.

There was no time to think or do anything else.

It was 8:45 a.m. The date was September 11 2001.

2

England, 2006

The TV crew from the BBC Look North studio were on hand purely by chance. One minute they were setting up to film a routine interview with a world-famous business consultant, in town to address a national conference; the next they were sprawled on the carpeted floor after an ear-shattering explosion rocked the very foundations of the building.

They were lucky; they were in a convention room at the back of the hotel, with a heavy projection screen between them and the windows, which shattered in the blast and sent lethal shards of glass hurtling in every direction.

It was only when they picked themselves up and ran out onto the quayside that they saw the extent of the damage, and the cost in human lives.

The bomber had chosen to detonate his device at the very centre of the Gateshead Millennium Bridge. The steel structure was pitted and scarred and dented from one side to the other; it looked as though a huge hand had punched into the tubular sections with ferocious power.

On both sides of the Tyne, the multi-windowed buildings, the pride of Newcastle and Gateshead, resembled nothing more than those in a war zone. Every huge window in the Baltic Art Gallery was gone, destroyed either by the nuts and bolts projected by the ten-pound IED, which had spewed out with the velocity of heavy machine-gun bullets, or by the sheer percussive force of the explosion.

But most terrifying of all were the bodies. The bomber had chosen his moment well. Dozens of businessmen and women, in Newcastle for the first time, had been taking a morning stroll from one side of the bridge to the other, getting some good Tyneside air before their conference began. It was 0830 hours; locals were crossing the bridge on their way to work, just as they did every morning.

Now they lay in grotesque, twisted shapes on the bridge and on the quayside. Those who had been closest to the suicide bomber had been hurled from the bridge into the cold, dark Tyne and were floating lifelessly in the water.

As the news reporter and cameraman ran from the hotel into the scene of devastation, they came to a standstill at the first horrifying sight of the carnage. Vehicles had skidded to a halt; drivers were running to help. There were moans and screams from the injured and, in the distance, the first police siren could be heard.

Then the reporter shouted to his ashen-faced colleague. 'Start shooting!' There was no response: the cameraman just stood and stared. 'Richie! Shoot it! Come on!'

With trembling hands the cameraman raised his camera and began to record the scene of horror. Within a day his footage, heavily edited, would be seen on television screens in every corner of the globe.

Black Star had struck again.

*   *   *

Elena's PC screen flicked into life; contact was re-established.

SO HOW YOU DOIN', GOLA?

THE SAME. I SAW WHAT HAPPENED IN NEWCASTLE. HE WAS SO BRAVE.

ALL MY ANGELS ARE BRAVE, GOLA, THEY GOTTA BE. WE TRAVEL A LONG ROAD BEFORE THEY'RE READY TO TAKE THE FINAL STEP TO FREEDOM.

YES, I SEE THAT MORE AND MORE. I SORT OF ENVIED HIM WHEN IT WAS ALL OVER.

WHY'S THAT, GOLA? TELL ME???

BECAUSE EVERYTHING SEEMS POINTLESS. STILL NO NEWS OF DAD, HE'S RUN OUT ON ME AGAIN. EVERYONE'S LET ME DOWN ALL MY LIFE.

YEAH, I KNOW THE FEELING.

IT'S NEVER REALLY BEEN RIGHT SINCE MUM DIED. WHY IS EVERYTHING SO UNFAIR?

CAN'T ANSWER THAT, GOLA, JUST KNOW IT IS FOR PEOPLE LIKE US. BUT ARE YOU REALLY READY TO DO SOMETHING ABOUT IT???? MAKE A DIFFERENCE, LIKE WE SAID?????? YOU AND ME HAVE COME A LONG WAY, TOO, BUT IN A SHORT TIME.

10

Elena turned away from her laptop screen and looked at Danny to her right, and then at Marcie Deveraux, who was sitting on her left.

'Be careful,' said Deveraux. 'You know what to say. Exactly as we've discussed, and nothing more.'

Elena nodded and her hands went back to the keyboard.

I THINK I'M READY.

There was a short delay before the next pop-up appeared on Elena's screen.

THINKING ISN'T ENOUGH. YOU'VE GOTTA BE CERTAIN BEFORE YOU TAKE THAT ULTIMATE STEP.

Deveraux leaned closer to Elena. When she spoke, her voice was insistent, but calm and assured.

'Ask the question. Just as I told you. And maintain contact and keep him online for as long as you can.'

Elena hit the keys again.

BUT WHAT ABOUT YOU??? WOULD YOU DO IT???

THOUGHT YOU'D ASK THAT!! AND I WILL DO IT, WHEN THE TIME IS RIGHT. BUT FOR NOW IT'S MY ROLE TO HELP OTHERS, LIKE THE ONES WHO'VE GONE BEFORE. LOOK, I UNDERSTAND COMPLETELY IF IT'S TOO MUCH FOR YA. THERE ARE OTHERS OUT THERE WAITING.

'Don't ask about the others,' said Deveraux quickly. 'Keep it on you, and your commitment.'

Elena nodded and took a deep breath. Just writing about what Black Star was proposing was enough to make her shiver. But she nodded again and began to type.

NO, I AM SURE. I'M CERTAIN!!! I'VE HAD ENOUGH! I WANNA SHOW EVERYONE EXACTLY WHAT I THINK OF THIS CRAP WORLD!!!

There was a longer delay, and Elena glanced anxiously at Deveraux. This was usually a sign that Black Star was about to close down.

'Maintain contact,' said Deveraux quickly. 'Ask about his real name. He knows yours. Ask him!'

But before Elena could begin to type, Black Star came back on screen.

OK. GOTTA GO NOW. WE'LL TALK AGAIN VERY SOON, MAKE PLANS. THIS CRAP WORLD'S GONNA DISCOVER WHAT A SPECIAL PERSON YOU ARE, GOLA!!!!!!!!!!

The screen went blank. Black Star had gone, and as Elena sat back in her chair, her hands were trembling.

Deveraux picked up her 'secure speech' Xda mobile, tapped the screen and put the device to her ear. She glared at Elena. 'You should have kept him online. The longer we have contact, the more chance there is of locating him.'

12

'We don't even know Black Star is a *he*,' said Danny, springing to the defence of his friend. 'And it's not Elena's fault if you can't find the target.'

'It's a man, I know it's a man,' said Deveraux over the ring tone in her ear.

Her call was answered. 'No good,' said a voice without waiting for the question. 'He's spoofed his ID through the Philippines and Berlin. We'll never find him like this.'

Deveraux hung up, turned to Fergus Watts and shook her head.

They were getting nowhere. In the four weeks since Elena had been making regular contact, Black Star, or the 'target', as the shadowy Internet figure was now termed, had never once disclosed a single personal detail: gender, age, location. Nothing.

Fergus was sitting in a wheelchair. He still wasn't used to it; it was almost as bad as being cooped up in a prison cell. Around his neck dangled the earpiece lead of a mini iPod. He had surprised Danny when he'd bought it three weeks earlier, saying it would give him something to do during any down time they had. He'd chosen the smallest and cheapest model, an iPod Shuffle, and it had accompanied him everywhere since Danny had shown him how to load it with the old rock music he liked.

He looked over at his grandson. 'Why don't you and Elena go outside for a while? Get some air. You've both been stuck in here for too long.'

The two teenagers needed no second invitation; they too had begun to feel like prisoners.

The room being used as the operational base was small and tucked away at the back of a hotel

13

just outside Oxford. The hotel was Danny and Elena's ACA, and their cover story was that they were living and working there. The living bit was true enough, but their work had nothing to do with the hotel.

The small hotel, used mainly as an overnight crash pad for sales reps during the week and for budget-conscious tourists visiting the university city at weekends, was owned by a couple who had taken early retirement from the Security Service. Like many such places, it was used occasionally by MI5 when they needed a safe and completely secure base for one or more operators.

Fergus waited until Danny and Elena had left the room before speaking to Deveraux. 'What is it with you? Is this how you're trained to run your people?'

Deveraux frowned and shook her head. 'What are you talking about?'

'Elena! You're not going to get results if you push her like that. She's young—she's not like one of your operatives. She's the only lead you've got to Black Star, but she's going to lose it if you don't lay off!'

Fergus's outburst had no effect on Deveraux; she was as calm and assured as ever as she went over to the coffee pot standing on a table in one corner of the room. She slowly and deliberately poured herself a full cup. 'I'm only interested in the mission, not in making friends.'

'Friends?' said Fergus, moving the wheelchair closer. 'I doubt if you've ever had a friend in your life. You're obsessive, like a machine. *All* you think about is the work.'

Deveraux's smile was not one of friendship.

14

'Like you?' For a few moments they stared at each other, both recognizing and silently acknowledging the similarities that made them so good at what they did. The best. But neither of them would have chosen to work together.

'Look, we didn't want to have anything to do with this job,' said Fergus. 'It was you and your boss who forced Elena into believing she was the only one who could get to Black Star. All that emotional blackmail stuff: *she* was his only known contact; *she* could help save so many innocent lives; the old "your country needs you" crap!'

Deveraux was unimpressed. 'You're making my heart bleed, Watts. Just remember, you and Danny are only part of this mission because Elena insisted on it.'

'Yeah,' said Fergus as he continued staring into Deveraux's eyes. 'And it's fortunate for us she did, isn't it? Because you and me both know what the alternative would have been.'

Deveraux didn't reply. There was no need. All that had saved them was the fact the Elena was the only person known to have made contact with Black Star.

Now Deveraux and Fergus were allies, reluctant allies, thrown together with one common aim.

'Just lay off a bit,' said Fergus. 'Elena's worried about her dad—and that creep she has to deal with day after day.' He watched as Deveraux took a sip of her coffee and then glanced towards the window.

'Joey's disappearance . . .' said Fergus quietly. 'There's nothing more you want to tell me about that, is there?'

Deveraux turned and looked straight at Fergus. 'No—nothing. From what I understand, he was always completely unreliable.'

'Was?'

Deveraux smiled again. 'Figure of speech.'

3

At first, on 9/11, Charles Pointer II had shared the numbing sense of disbelief with millions of others around the world as he watched the horrific scenes of aircraft slamming into the Twin Towers replayed over and over again on television.

He didn't know what his son was doing or where he was on that day, so after a while he called his mobile. There was no answer. He wasn't particularly worried: mobile networks were down and the whole country was in a state of confusion. And anyway, as far as Pointer knew, Chuck had no reason to be downtown.

But after trying the mobile throughout the afternoon and into the early evening, a nightmare scenario began to take shape in Pointer's mind. He went into his son's bedroom and reluctantly began to search through the desk next to the bed. He felt a little guilty as he began to fumble hesitantly through the drawers. He had always, until this moment, respected Chuck's privacy.

He found the neatly typed envelope bearing a blue company logo in the central drawer of the desk. It was addressed to his son, and as Charles Pointer II took out the perfectly folded letter, he saw that his hands were trembling.

The paper was expensive, with a watermark. In one corner was the same blue company logo, and

16

beneath the logo was the name Hanover, a British finance company, with the address of its New York offices. Pointer's heart tightened in his chest.

He read the short, businesslike letter inviting his son for an interview that morning at 9 a.m.

At that moment he knew. Chuck, his beloved seventeen-year-old son, was dead.

Pointer's legs felt as though they could no longer support him and he sank down onto Chuck's bed. He stared at the letter, but he was no longer seeing the words. Instead, the horrifying images he had watched throughout the day came back into his mind. The planes, the flames, victims hurling themselves to their death, the Twin Towers collapsing one after another, the billowing black smoke and dust enveloping whole blocks of the city.

He had no idea how long he sat on the bed, staring at the letter, but eventually the words on the page came into focus again. He re-read the letter, and his eyes fixed on the last line before the 'Yours sincerely' and the signature: 'I look forward to seeing you.'

'I look forward to seeing you,' he whispered. But Charles Pointer II could never again look forward to seeing his precious son. Not in this lifetime.

The printed words began to blur on the paper, and Pointer eventually realized that they were slowly dissolving, being washed away. By his own silent tears.

Chuck's body was never identified, or, like hundreds of others, it was simply never found. The memorial service was simple, dignified. Some of Chuck's schoolfriends; a few very old and very distant relatives; some business associates.

Charles Pointer II was now alone. His wife had died four years earlier and since then—before then, if he was totally honest with himself—all his love and energy had been channelled towards his son's welfare and future. Now there was no future.

*   *   *

In the days, weeks and months that followed, the USA and the rest of the world attempted to come to terms with the enormity of the outrage committed on 9/11.

'Life must go on,' said many of the family and friends of the victims. 'They would want us to go on. To remember them, but to go on.'

But Charles Pointer II never came to terms with what had happened. First he was overwhelmed by grief, then grief gave way to anger, and then that anger grew to an all-consuming rage—and a quest for revenge. And then Pointer began making his plans.

The family business was easy to sell, particularly as it went for a knockdown price. But that still meant many millions of dollars, far more than Pointer would ever need.

Once the deal was concluded, Pointer retreated to his summer home in The Hamptons. The long stretch of coastline was just a couple of hours away from Manhattan and was famed as the playground of New York's rich and famous.

Pointer's mock-Gothic mansion, surrounded by high chain-link fencing and even higher gate, became his fortress. The doors were locked and the shutters at the windows were closed and secured. From then on he never left the safety and sanctuary of his fortress, and only ever had face-to-face contact with one man.

Herman Ramirez had turned up at the Pointers' summer home some fifteen years earlier, offering his services as a gardener and general handyman. There were no references—Herman had arrived in the US as an illegal immigrant from Mexico several years before that.

Pointer had almost sent him packing. But something about the quietly spoken, polite but determined Mexican made him stop and listen. Herman explained that he was a good gardener, had trained as a mechanic in Mexico, was hardworking and trustworthy.

Pointer believed him, and he remembered the Pointer family motto: initiative and determination. He took him on, part-time at first, but Herman soon made himself indispensable. For the first five years he travelled in every day from his tenement room in New York. Occasionally, when there was a lot to do, he would stay over in the small separate annexe.

Eventually he just moved in. For good. Not just because he had become a loyal and trusted member of the Pointer household, but also because he'd become a firm friend and favourite of young Chuck.

He was now one of the family. He had no family of his own—or none that he had ever mentioned—and he treated Chuck as if he were his own son. At Chuck's memorial service Pointer and Herman had stood side by side, weeping silently.

Now they met when it was necessary. Pointer would summon him by mobile and Herman would use his key to the back door of the darkened house.

Then he would wait until his master emerged from the gloom. They would discuss what was necessary, what was required, and then go back to their separate tasks. They never spoke about Chuck; there was nothing more they could say.

From the outside, the house and grounds looked just as they always had. Neat, tidy, well-clipped hedges, fir trees and trimmed lawns.

Inside, it was totally different. Changed completely, like its owner. Most of the rooms were no longer used; they simply gathered dust behind closed curtains and fixed shutters. The few rooms Pointer inhabited in the eastern wing of the grand building never saw daylight. The decorative chandeliers were never switched on. Pointer moved around and operated in nothing more than the light from a single small lamp. Darkness had enveloped his soul. His world was darkness too.

Pointer's rage against the world was all-consuming. Families like his were the backbone of the country; they were the moneymakers, the employers, the sort of family that had made America great. But now it had ended; the last of the line was dead. And Pointer blamed not just Al Qaeda, Osama Bin Laden or Muslim extremists in general. He blamed the whole world. The warmongers, the arms sellers, the empire builders, the Americans, the British. Black, white, Muslim, Christian, Jew. The entire world and everyone in it was responsible for snatching away Pointer's beloved son, and the entire world would have to pay.

However long it took, Charles Pointer III—Charlie Three, Chuck—would be avenged.

4

The brush-contact exercise needed to be repeated and perfected after the dismal showing Danny and Elena had put on the last time they had attempted it.

The failure was mainly down to Elena, although Danny had blamed himself when Fergus gave them a hard time during the debrief back at the hotel. But Elena was having none of it: it was her cock-up; it was up to her to get it right.

'It's up to both of you to get it right,' Fergus had told them. 'You're a team, *we're* a team, and a mistake by one could lead to the death of another. So, first and foremost, we're looking out for each other. Got it?'

They both nodded. When he put it like that, the full realization of what they had agreed to be part of hit home. Hard.

Fergus had lived by the seven Ps maxim—Prior Planning and Preparation Prevents Piss Poor Performance—during his years in the SAS, and nothing was going to change now.

But the training had to be quick and intense— there was no knowing when Black Star would decide he had groomed Elena sufficiently for her to carry out an attack. Every effort was being made to trace the whereabouts of Black Star's lair, but so far they had found nothing.

With each passing day it seemed more likely that Black Star would move Elena on to an attack phase. She hadn't been in regular contact with him for long, but she seemed to be convincing him that she was as disillusioned with life as the other teenagers he had picked to carry out his terrible revenge. When he decided to go ahead, Marcie Deveraux was convinced that he would have to reveal more information to her; information that would ultimately lead to his downfall.

Elena had agreed to be in the front line of the battle to get Black Star, but *only* if Danny was there in support. And despite Deveraux's misgivings, she had to concede that in operational terms it made perfect sense. Elena would have to pass on information if the operation went into a second phase; it would be far less conspicuous if she were working with someone of her own age.

So Danny and Elena both had to be trained and prepared, and both had insisted that Fergus handle that training. Again, Deveraux couldn't argue. There was no one better at preparing for covert work than Fergus Watts. It had been his entire life: his attention to detail was absolute; *he* was the expert.

One of Fergus's first orders was that when and if they did move into the second phase, there would be no form of electronic communication between Elena and the others. Black Star was a proven master of technology: one slip-up with a mobile phone or e-mail could lead to disaster.

So it was back to the old ways of tradecraft. There was a lot to learn, and Fergus was using the city of Oxford as Danny and Elena's training ground. Every test was carried out amongst the third party, and third party meant everyone not involved in the exercise: shoppers, shopkeepers, traffic wardens, even the police. If either of the teenagers made a mistake, the third party could easily notice. And if the third party could, Black Star most certainly would.

For now, any mistakes could be rectified. Even if an exercise went badly wrong and Danny and Elena ended up being pulled by the police, it could be sorted by Deveraux. Her MI5 clearance was so high that even chief constables would jump at her command.

But it wouldn't be like that with Black Star.

Oxford city centre was less busy than Danny had hoped. It meant the W H Smith store would not be jam-packed with shoppers, and that would make the brush-contact test even more difficult.

The test sounded simple, but it had done on the previous occasion too. As before, they were to carry out a brush contact in which Danny received a small plastic tub—the type usually containing 35mm camera film—from Elena without the operation being spotted by the third party.

The last time they had tried the drill, Elena had dropped the canister at the very moment she was meant to pass it to Danny. It had bounced onto the floor and another shopper had picked it up and given it back to Elena while Danny walked on. That was it: there were no second attempts once the move had failed.

This time they had to get it right.

Elena was the sponsor of the operation; meaning she had planned the contact. It was likely that if this happened for real, she would be the one making decisions on the ground, passing on information she had gathered about the 'target'. Danny would never be in overt contact with her. As far as Black Star was concerned, Elena was on her own.

She had left her brush-contact orders at a DLB she had chosen earlier: the gap behind a washbasin in Starbucks. Danny had collected the orders and was walking through the city centre shopping precinct. He kept his head down, but not too much—just enough to avoid the direct line of the CCTV cameras. The whole idea was to look natural and avoid arousing suspicion. He was feeling nervous: training was going far from perfectly, and his grandfather was never happy with anything less than perfection.

Danny and Elena had set their watches to the time check on BBC Radio Four earlier that morning. It was vital that both watches were perfectly synchronized as the brush contact they were about to carry out depended on split-second timing. Danny checked his watch: it read 12:06 p.m.

Four minutes to go. At precisely 12:10 Danny was due to brush past Elena in W H Smith and take from her right hand the small plastic tub. On this occasion the tub would be empty, but if they ever got to do this for real, it might contain vital information such as the real name of Black Star, or even his whereabouts.

Danny checked his watch again as he pushed through the glass entrance doors of W H Smith. Less than three minutes to go and there were very few shoppers in the store, which was not good. The busier the better for cover.

Elena had chosen the CD department for the contact. It was a good choice: teenagers blended in naturally there. But security was tight, with CCTV cameras and uniformed security guards. And the guards were not only on the lookout for shoplifters: since the suicide bombing campaign had begun,

24

there was heightened security everywhere.

The DLB instructions had told Danny to go to the rap section in the CD department and to check out the CDs beginning with the letter F. With a minute and a half to go Danny picked up a 50 Cent CD and tried to look as natural as possible as he read the track list. He put the CD back in the rack and flicked through a few more.

A uniformed guard gave Danny no more than a glance as he passed by; Danny was experienced enough now to avoid obvious errors like wearing a bulky jacket or carrying a rucksack. He checked his watch again: fifteen seconds to go. He hadn't once looked for Elena; the instruction was that at exactly 12.10 p.m. she would be looking through the CDs at the end of the rack, to his right. He began to mentally count down the final seconds, adding a thousand to each digit—Fergus had told them many times that this was the way to slow down a count when you were nervous. Thousand and one, thousand and two, thousand and three . . .

He reached one thousand and fifteen and looked to his right. Elena was there, just six metres away, and turning towards him. But three more CD browsers were now between them.

It didn't matter; they both knew exactly what to do. They stepped away from the rack and began walking towards each other, not making eye contact. The rule was, never give the slightest clue that you know each other.

Danny passed the first browser as Elena slipped round the girl closest to her. The brush contact was on, although at any stage, if either of them felt the operation was not secure, they could abort by turning back to the CD racks. The other would

25

then walk straight on by.

Two metres to go and Danny could see the film container in Elena's right hand. He slightly relaxed the fingers of his own right hand so that, as they passed each other, he would be ready to receive the small tub.

He stepped around the final browser just as Elena brushed past. Their hands touched, and the canister passed smoothly from one to the other.

But there was no time for celebration. On covert operations there always had to be a reason for being wherever you were, whether the operation had been a success or a failure.

Danny remembered his instructions and went to the newspaper stands, where he picked up a copy of the *Sun*, and then joined the queue for the cash desk.

As he stood waiting to pay, he saw Fergus being pushed in his wheelchair towards the desk by Marcie Deveraux. Neither of them looked at Danny, but he was aware that they knew exactly what had happened.

He handed over the correct change and left the shop, clutching his newspaper and allowing himself the slightest of smiles.

5

Pointer's skin had become almost translucent, like a fish that hugs the inky darkness of the deepest ocean bed where no light ever penetrates.

Only his cheeks and forehead showed any colour: they were a vivid, veiny red. But the redness was no early warning of high blood pressure or stress. Pointer was always calm now. His heartbeat was still normal, even though everything else about him had changed. The redness on his face came from the hours he spent sitting in the darkness in front of his computer screen. As Pointer stared at the screen, the screen stared back, gradually etching its imprint onto his face.

Computer technology and the Internet had been Pointer's life, and he had chosen the Internet as his method of operation. And as his teenage son had been taken away, he chose other teenagers as the foot soldiers in his war of revenge.

They were not easy to find, but he found them. He ventured into the Web, searching for the depressed, the disaffected, the disillusioned. He looked in on chat sites, learning the language of the young. Computer speak. Techno talk.

He began his painstakingly slow and ultra-cautious search for potential collaborators, moving gradually to the most obscure Internet sites. Suicide chat rooms and suicide cults. He quickly identified and rejected the merely bored kids seeking some excitement, and those rebelling against over-protective parents, or the broken-hearted recently dumped by a girl- or boyfriend. And Pointer was far too skilled for any watchdog police officers posing online as teenagers. He knew exactly who to avoid. And who to target.

And when he identified his targets, he struck. He went only for English speakers: if it was not their native tongue, they had to be fluent in the language. Black Star could not afford any misunderstandings. Slowly and carefully he entered into online communication, beginning by sending pop-ups onto their computer screens.

Some, he helped, when there was a problem that could be solved by his special computer skills. And once he had helped, and they were in his debt, he took the next step, entering into actual online conversations, commiserating with the disaffected, cultivating the disillusioned and depressed, sowing the seeds of his plan. Only when he was completely sure did he introduce the theme of suicide. And one by one, Pointer—now calling himself Black Star—recruited his foot soldiers.

The first bombings had taken place in England, partly because that was where the first and strongest contacts had been made. But it also seemed like justice to Black Star, because Chuck had been on his way to an interview with an English finance company when he was killed. England was Black Star's testing ground, but after the Newcastle bombing it was time to move on to other parts of the world.

Black Star had followed the news reports of the British bombings on the Internet and the American television news. He was pleased to see that the British press had begun referring to his bombers as 'Angels of Death'.

They were his 'Angels of Death' and there were more in waiting. His recruits were few in number; there could never be legions of young people committed enough to walk willingly to their deaths. But further recruits were being cultivated and were almost ready for the final order. They waited in many countries of the world. In Canada, Australia, New Zealand, Pakistan and Israel among others. And, of course, they waited in the USA. But for the USA, Black Star was grooming one very special

28

Angel of Death.

6

Elena was in the hotel garden, having just finished one of her regular sessions with psychiatrist Dr Ruth Jacobson.

She didn't mind the sessions, and she knew precisely why she and the doctor were having these regular 'little chats'. Marcie Deveraux couldn't afford for her to crack up. One impulsive response to a provocative comment and Elena could easily give the game away and ruin the entire operation.

And once out on the ground, if they ever got that far, it would be even more difficult as Elena would be beyond direct control.

So she was being closely monitored.

Elena liked Dr Jacobson. In some ways she reminded her of Jane Brooker, the woman who ran Foxcroft residential home with her husband Dave. Jane loved a good old chat over a cup of tea, especially with some of the older girls.

Jane was straight and honest, and Elena instinctively knew that Dr Jacobson was too. Unlike Deveraux. Elena would never trust Deveraux.

During the session Elena had spoken a lot about how she missed her dad. He had disappeared again just when she thought they were, at last, beginning to understand each other and forge a proper relationship.

'The trouble is,' she said to Dr Jacobson, 'even if he is trying to contact me now, there's no way he can find me. They made up this story for the people at Foxcroft and social services. So Dad wouldn't know how to reach me.' Her usually bright face suddenly became hard and distant. 'But knowing Dad, he's probably not given me a single thought since he walked out again.'

The session wound up and Elena went out into the garden to think through everything they had spoken about. She was sitting on a bench, watching a gang of sparrows noisily fighting over some breadcrumbs thrown onto the grass by the hotel chef, when Danny emerged from the side door and came strolling over.

He smiled. 'All right?'

Elena raised her eyebrows. 'Not really.'

Danny sat on the bench. 'Why? Has the fruit doctor been giving you a hard time?'

'It's nothing to do with Dr Jacobson,' said Elena coldly as the battle for the breadcrumbs ended and the sparrows flew away. She turned to look at Danny. 'It's you!'

'Me? What have I done?'

'D'you know what day it was yesterday?'

'Yeah . . . Wednesday.'

Elena sighed and shook her head. 'It was my birthday. Thanks for remembering.'

Danny's eyes widened. 'Was it?'

'You didn't forget last year. But then you weren't totally obsessed by all this stuff, like you are now.'

'I'm really sorry, Elena.'

'I didn't get one card. Not *one*! I never expected anyone else to think of it, but I thought you'd remember.'

'I'll go and get you a present. Today.'

'I don't want a stupid present. Not now—it's too

30

late.'

They sat in silence for a moment, Elena still angry and Danny considering what she had said about him being obsessed by the mission. 'Look, once this is over we'll go back to how it was. I'll get a job, you'll do your A-levels, and then—'

'It'll never be over, Danny,' said Elena angrily. 'Not for you. You love it, you know you do. I see it every time your granddad sets us one of his tests. You want to be as good as him. You want to *be* him.'

It was true, he realized that. And it wasn't just this mission; the whole clandestine world of the Secret Service was fascinating and exciting. He felt part of it, as though he belonged. For years he had dreamed of a career as an army officer. But this was something else. Something more. Something in which he felt there was scope to be not just a team player, but also an individual.

And however much Danny tried to follow orders and instructions, there was a part of him that needed to be the individual, to make his own decisions, right or wrong.

But Elena was special to him—he knew that too. And he had messed up big time. 'I'm sorry, really I am. But what we're doing is important.'

'I know it's important, I'm not stupid. But you were the one who wanted this sort of life, not me. I had everything planned. A-levels, university, a great job as a computer scientist.'

Elena sighed with irritation and then stood up and started back towards the hotel. But then she stopped and turned round. 'What I did before was for *you*, you and your granddad. I never wanted to be part of something like this.'

31

'But we are,' said Danny. 'There's no going back now.'

Elena nodded. 'I know. But when it's over, I want a . . . a normal life.'

Danny stood up. 'Look, I'll always be there for you, Elena. I promise.'

Elena shook her head and smiled. Her anger had gone. 'Yeah. And I bet you forget my birthday next year too.'

7

Jeff Williams and Kiyoshi Tanaka had never met and were separated by 6,619 miles, but they had much in common.

They were both just eighteen, they both lived at home with their parents and they were both computer science students. And the two teenagers also shared a passion with many thousands of others around the world. Trains. They were real-life train-spotters.

Maybe it was the model train sets they had both been given as children that had sparked the initial love of trains in both boys. But there was another element to train-spotting that suited both Jeff and Kiyoshi: it was a solitary pastime. And both teenagers were regarded as loners. Outsiders. Not one of the gang. They had both put up with their fair share of bullying over the years. Nothing too terrible; nothing like being regularly beaten up. But it was the constant drip, drip, drip of ridicule and sarcasm that had ground them down. Made them hate life. Made them want to get their own back on a hostile world . . .

Jeff's particular interest was freight trains. He would spend hours watching the seemingly endless trains, with their double engines front and back, snake their way around the hills overlooking Pittsburgh. He would check engine numbers, count the freight wagons, note the type of freight and write everything down in a little book. He never ceased to wonder at the fact that the trains were so long that the front section had crossed Pittsburgh and disappeared into the hills while the rear trucks were still on the other side of the city.

Kiyoshi's special fascination was for the sleek, aerodynamic, high-speed trains that carried up to four million people a day in and out of Tokyo's Shinjuku Station.

Both teenagers had told Black Star about their love of trains and railways during their early online conversations. And it was their enthusiasm that had given Black Star the ghoulish idea of devising and preparing their suicides for exactly the same moment.

A synchronized act of terrorism was right and fitting for Black Star, as it was the synchronized act of terrorism on 9/11 that had sparked the quest for revenge.

So, at 7:30 a.m., as the early commuters began spilling from a train at Shinjuku Station, Kiyoshi went to the middle of the platform, pulled the twine in his right hand and exploded the device strapped to his body.

Jeff's suicide had actually taken place a few minutes earlier: the time in Pittsburgh was 6:24 p.m. It should have been equally spectacular. Jeff had picked the precise spot where he would lie down on the tracks and explode the device as the freight train approached. He knew the device would not be enough to destroy the train itself. But Jeff's bomb was going to blow away a whole section of the track. The approaching train would be derailed and much of it would then tumble down the hillside towards the city.

But Jeff got it wrong. He prepared the device, just as he had been instructed, strapped it to his body, and had the detonating twine ready. He borrowed his dad's car, drove off into the hills and found his parking spot.

As he switched off the car's engine, opened the driver's door and got out, something made him take the twine in his right hand and pull it gently, just to test the pressure.

But the pull was not gentle enough. The bomb exploded. A few minutes later, at exactly 6:30 p.m., the freight train began to pass by. The train driver looked out of his cab and saw the smouldering hulk of a burning Ford.

Jeff had simply disappeared. Later they found the remains of his body. And his notebook.

8

Deveraux's boss at MI5 arrived first thing the following morning and was swiftly in conversation behind a locked door with Deveraux, Fergus and Dr Jacobson.

Dudley—he was known only as Dudley, and few people in the Secret Service knew for certain whether it was his first or his second name—was the one who had convinced Danny and Elena that their help with the mission was vital. They hadn't seen him since then. They were unlikely to see him now.

He tossed a copy of the *Mirror* onto the desk. Its headline was similar to the ones splashed across the front page of every other daily newspaper.

ANGELS OF DEATH
STRIKE AGAIN

'We must move this on now, sir,' said Deveraux urgently. 'We have to get Elena to push Black Star into giving us more to go on. We know now that these kids are making the devices themselves. Something Black Star tells Elena will give us the clues we need.'

The air in the operations room was already stale and heavy. The desktops were cluttered with empty coffee cups, discarded newspapers and opened files of the most recent data.

'I'm aware of your views, Marcie,' said Dudley. 'But I have to take into consideration other opinions.' He looked at the psychiatrist. 'Doctor, is there any more you can tell us about Black Star?'

Dr Ruth Jacobson's regular presence at the hotel had a dual purpose. Not only was she overseeing Elena's emotional welfare and ensuring she wasn't succumbing to Black Star's grooming, she was also attempting to put together a psychological profile of the bomb master. It was a major part of her job, and during her career she had helped police and the security services to track down a number of highly dangerous criminals, ranging from serial killers to terrorists.

There were those within the police and the security services who regarded her work as a waste of both time and resources and thought that her success was based on little more than lucky hunches and educated guesses. But others—and fortunately they were in the majority—knew the full value of Ruth Jacobson's incisive mind.

Since Elena had resumed her online conversations with Black Star, Dr Jacobson had been fully involved, studying transcripts of the conversations and analysing every single word in her attempt to form a picture of the bomb master.

'I'm fairly certain now that Black Star is a man,' she said, leafing through the transcripts.

Deveraux looked unimpressed. 'I've known that all along.'

Dr Jacobson was not thrown by Deveraux's dismissive attitude; she was fully aware that the high-flying MI5 agent was one of the sceptics. 'But I think now that he's not a young man. He's middle aged, at least.'

Deveraux suddenly seemed interested. 'And what makes you think that?'

Dr Jacobson put the papers she was holding down on the desk. 'For a start he seems . . . experienced. And some of the phrases he uses—they're more . . . mature.'

She pointed to a line in the typed transcript of the last conversation. 'Look at this. He says, "It's my *role* to help others." *Role* is an unusual word these days. I think a young man would have said "job". And look here, in the next sentence. He says, "I understand completely." It's grammatically correct, but most people today would say, "I completely understand"—particularly young people. There are other examples in earlier conversations.'

Deveraux said nothing for a moment as she tried to form her own mental picture of a middle-aged man, sitting in front of a computer screen somewhere in the world, luring teenagers to their deaths. It was irritating to admit to herself that Dr Jacobson was probably right. 'Sick bastard, whoever he is.'

'Mentally disturbed, certainly. Perhaps unhinged in some way by a catastrophe in his own life.'

'Are you asking me to feel sorry for him?' snapped Deveraux.

'I'm giving you my professional opinion,' replied Dr Jacobson calmly. 'My thinking at the moment is that he's carefully learned to converse online like young people. To make them feel as though they're communicating with one of their own. But personal history always leaves its traces.'

Dudley nodded. 'Have you said anything to Elena about this?'

Dr Jacobson glanced at Fergus and then at Deveraux before replying. 'No. Elena is a remarkable young girl, but we have to remember her age and the fact that she's gone through an extremely traumatic time over the past few years—losing her mother, then the business with her father . . .'

Fergus spotted the almost unnoticeable look that passed between Deveraux and Dudley.

'But you do feel she is strong enough to continue?' said Dudley to Dr Jacobson. 'And to carry this on to the second phase, if it is necessary?'

'As I said, she is a remarkable young woman. She's coping, but I have concerns.' She glanced at

Deveraux. 'She's doing OK for the moment, but some news of her father would help.'

'There is no news,' said Deveraux impatiently. 'Joey Omolodon is a loser. He's either lying low somewhere or has skipped the country.'

'Nevertheless, if you hear anything—'

'Then Elena will be the first to know. Now, can we get back to business.'

Dudley picked up his coffee cup and drank the last mouthful of the cold, bitter liquid. He grimaced as he placed the cup carefully back on its saucer. 'Should we put someone else at the computer? Danny perhaps?'

Dr Jacobson shook her head. 'Good idea, but it's too late now. Black Star would spot it immediately. He knows Elena's computer language. Everyone has their own unique way of abbreviating text, and if Danny stopped to think about Elena's way of replying, BS would smell a rat.'

Dudley nodded and then turned to Fergus. 'And your thoughts, Mr Watts?'

Fergus had trained raw recruits before. He knew exactly what was required out in the field. 'Operationally, neither Danny or Elena are ready. Sitting behind a computer is one thing, but being out on the ground is completely different. I need more time.'

Dudley sighed and glanced at the newspapers scattered about the desktop. 'Unfortunately time is one of the many things we do not have on our side. This is now a global situation. Other national security organizations will be taking their own measures, but for the moment it's been decided that we in this country keep what we know to ourselves. And make our own moves.'

He stood up and slowly and deliberately began to button up the overcoat he wore in almost all weathers. Fergus watched him, not for a single moment taken in by Dudley's gentlemanly ways and polite manners. No one got to his position in the Security Service by being Mister Nice Guy.

Dudley secured the top button and brushed away an invisible speck of dust from the collar of his coat. 'We take the risk,' he said. 'We get Elena to convince Black Star that she's completely ready to move on to the second stage. We must hope that that is enough to lure him into making a mistake.' He looked at Fergus. 'And my decision is final.'

9

The table in Fergus's room was laden with items from a shopping expedition to Tesco. Some of the plastic bottles and tubs remained unopened, but in the middle lay a pile of aspirin tablets.

Danny and Elena were sitting on one side, while Fergus stood on the other, leaning on the tabletop for extra support. His injured leg was getting stronger, but his recent gunshot wound had been in almost the identical place to one he had taken in Colombia nearly eight years earlier, so it was taking longer to heal. Every day his leg felt stronger and every day he pushed himself a little more. He could stand unaided now for a short time and even walk a few steps without crutches. But there was still a long way to go.

It was just after two in the afternoon and, as always, the day had been planned to make maximum use of every available hour. Elena usually made contact with Black Star in the early or mid evening. As far as Black Star was concerned, that was after she had finished her shift at the hotel. Mornings were for updates and debriefs and afternoons were for training.

'Show-and-tell time,' said Fergus as Danny and Elena eyed the bizarre assortment on the table.

Danny was staring at a large cooking pot. 'Are we cooking, then?'

'Something like that,' said Fergus. 'I'm going to show you a thing or two about plastic explosive.'

Danny's and Elena's eyes widened.

'These are the same everyday items that Black Star's Angels have used to make their PE.'

'You mean they made their bombs themselves?' said Elena.

'IEDs,' said Fergus, correcting her. 'I made one myself, remember? When we were in the warehouse—before we were dragged into this business. But I had proper PE to work with; the Angels are using a home-made variety.'

Danny and Elena listened in complete silence as Fergus explained that all versions of home-made explosive have a mix number, and that when he was in the Regiment he had learned to remember all the ingredients and recipes for every different mix.

Many of his covert jobs had involved going into enemy territory with no equipment at all. Once there, he would have to buy the ingredients—everyday items that would arouse no suspicion—to make HE.

Depending on the target—say a power station or a bridge—the mix number would be different, because each mix had a different detonation velocity. And some mixes were easier to make than others.

Fergus looked down at the items on the table. 'Forensic tests show that the Angels were using this stuff to make a PE called mix thirty-nine.'

Danny was staring at the ingredients with a new fascination, but Elena was looking worried. 'Are you saying I might have to make one of these IED things?'

Fergus nodded. 'It's possible, Elena. We don't know how far down the line you'll have to go with Black Star before we can get to him. After the attacks in Japan and America yesterday, we now know that Black Star doesn't meet with his Angels to make the IEDs, unless he has accomplices. My guess is that somehow he provides instructions on how to make them.'

'And that's what I'll have to do?'

Fergus was trying his best to be reassuring. 'Look, don't worry. I'll be giving you something to make the mixture safe.'

'Really?' said Elena, looking far from reassured. 'And what's that?'

'It's a . . . a powder. You'll mix it into all the ingredients you have here.'

'What sort of powder?'

'One step at a time. Thirty-nine is highly dangerous at the mixing stage and extremely volatile once it's made.'

'But you said the mixture will be safe.'

'And it will. But you need to be prepared for every eventuality. And even if you had to go through with making the PE for real, you could still make the device safe by detaching the det wires from the battery—although it'd still be unstable.'

41

He saw Elena's look of confusion and smiled reassuringly. 'Like I said, one step at a time. And we won't let it get that far.'

Elena and Danny sat back and listened as Fergus explained that the high explosive the ingredients made was a 'cousin' of TNT and was called Trinitrophenol. He pointed down at the aspirin on the tabletop. 'By extracting the Trinitrophenol from these little things and then mixing it with Vaseline and candles, anyone with the know-how can make their own plastic explosive within three hours.'

Danny was anxious to know more. 'So how's it done? Are we gonna make some mix thirty-nine now?'

'The aspirins are boiled down, and then some of the other ingredients are added to extract the Trinitrophenol. And no, we're not making it. Apart from anything else, the fumes are poisonous during the mixing.'

Elena was looking more and more concerned and Fergus could see it. 'Look, you just have to know about it—we'll probably get Black Star long before this stage.'

'Probably?'

Fergus was suddenly aware that his leg was aching badly. He moved slowly round to the other side of the table, pulled up a chair and sat between Danny and Elena.

He kept his voice low as he spoke. 'We can't step back from this now. We have the best chance there is to rid the world of this Black Star scum.' He leaned closer. 'But what I care about most is keeping you two safe.'

'You mean with the IED?' said Danny.

'Not just the IED.' Fergus deliberately spoke softly so that they were forced to lean in even closer to hear his words. 'We've got to tread very carefully around Deveraux. I never trusted her before and I still don't. She's only interested in getting Black Star. Once that's achieved, we become a problem again. So then, she has three options. One, she lets us walk away and get a life away from all this. Two, there's another job that we have no choice but to take. Or three . . .'

'She kills us,' breathed Danny.

Fergus nodded. 'And that seems the most likely option to me. So here's the plan. The moment Black Star is found and we've done our bit, you do only what *I* tell you. You ignore any further orders from Deveraux. I'll get us away to a safe place, and I'll make certain that Deveraux will never be able to hurt us.'

'But how can you do that?' said Danny urgently.

'I'm putting together a security blanket that will take care of us all. But just remember, once Black Star is found, you do exactly what I tell you.'

Fergus let the words sink in before speaking again. 'Any questions?'

'Yeah,' said Elena. 'Tell me about this powder that makes the IED safe.'

Fergus smiled. 'Don't worry. You'll know all about it when the time's right.'

10

Elena took a deep breath as she gathered her thoughts and began to type.

I READ ABOUT JAPAN AND AMERICA. THEY WERE AMAZING!!! THEY SHOWED THE WAY FOR US ALL!!!

She hesitated and her eyes flicked towards Danny and Dr Jacobson for reassurance. She was meant to write more but it was difficult.

'Go on,' urged Deveraux quickly. 'Tell him.'

Dr Jacobson glared at Deveraux, but wisely said nothing. The atmosphere in the operations room was already as tense as stretched wire.

Elena's fingers went back to the keyboard.

I CAN BE THAT BRAVE. I AM THAT BRAVE!!! I'M SO CERTAIN NOW!!!

The reply was instantaneous.

REALLY, GOLA? ABSOLUTELY CERTAIN???

Elena began to write swiftly, as though she was no longer thinking about each carefully placed word, as though her thoughts were just spilling out. Ignoring errors and spelling mistakes, she hammered the keys.

TOTALLY!!! DAD RUNNING OUT AGAIN WAS THE END FOR ME, IVE HAD ENOUGH!

I HATE HIM!! EVERYONE LETS ME DOWN, EVERYONE!!! IT WAS MY BIRTHDAY THE OTHER WEEK AND NORT EVEN MY BEST FRIEND REMEMBERED!!!

She kept pounding away at the keyboard, knowing that Danny was looking at her.

YOURE THE ONLY PERSON WHO TALKS STRAIUGHJT TO ME. I WANT OUT, REALLY! COMPELETLY, TOTALLY, FOR GOOD!!! AND I WANNA MAKE THEM ALL SORRY FOR ALL THE SHIT THEYVE GIVEN ME FOR TOO LONG!! SHOW ME THE WAY, PLEASE!!!!!!!!!!!!!!!!!!!!!!!!!!

Elena sat back, her eyes wide as she waited for Black Star's response. The others were all staring at her. She'd gone off script; she'd gone further than she'd been instructed, but Deveraux was delighted. 'Good, Elena, very good. The birthday was brilliant, and telling him the way you feel about your father was excellent.'

'Just *piss* off,' hissed Elena, still staring at the screen.

Deveraux glanced towards Fergus, who was glaring at her accusingly. She held the stare for a moment but then returned to the computer screen.

*   *   *

Charles Pointer II had invited his faithful servant Herman Ramirez into the gloom of his huge mansion in The Hamptons to witness him reeling in the latest and most highly prized Angel.

45

'I have her,' he whispered without looking away from his computer screen. 'My first female Angel. Everything she's told me has checked out. The father in jail and then disappearing, the residential home, and now this dead-end hotel job. She's perfect, and her timing is perfect. Exactly when I need her—and I have no need to push. She's mine, and no one is watching over her.'

'Only you, sir,' said Herman as his master reverted to his Black Star persona.

I'LL SHOW YOU THE WAY, GOLA. AND I'M SO PROUD OF YA!!! I'LL START MAKING ARRANGEMENTS. YOU'RE GONNA MAKE A DIFFERENCE AND BE FAMOUS!!! YOU GOT A PASSPORT???

In the operations room at the hotel there was a sudden moment of confusion. No one had been expecting a question like this—the other Angels had killed themselves in their own countries. Elena looked anxiously at Fergus and then at Deveraux.

'Do you?' said Deveraux.

Elena shook her head.

'Say you do. Tell him you have a passport.'

'No!' said Fergus. 'Tell him the truth.' He looked at Deveraux. 'He can hack into secure sites. Lie to him now and he just might go and discover the truth for himself. Details—keep thinking details or we get caught out.'

Deveraux realized that Fergus was right. She nodded at Elena to continue.

SORRY, NO. I'VE NEVER BEEN OUT OF THIS COUNTRY. SAD, OR WHAT?

46

NO WAY ARE U SAD, GOLA, NO WAY. BUT THE PASSPORT IS THE ONE THING YOU GOTTA ORGANIZE. AND QUICKLY. THAT'S ALL YOU HAVE 2 DO. WILL YOU DO IT???

'Tell him you will,' said Fergus.

NO PROBLEM, I CAN SORT IT.

GREAT!!! LEAVE EVERYTHING ELSE 2 ME, EVERYTHING! I'LL HAVE SUMTHING FOR U VERY SOON. BYE FOR NOW!!!!!!

Black Star was gone and Elena quickly logged off.

Danny turned to Deveraux. 'What about me? I haven't got a passport.'

'We can arrange it. We can arrange everything.'

'But Elena must go through the proper channels,' said Fergus. 'Passport Office, countersignature—I think we'd better get Dave Brooker to do that; none of us can sign the form without possibly alerting Black Star. Everything has to be done properly.'

Deveraux nodded. 'You were right back there. It was quick thinking.' She made for the door but stopped short and glanced back at Fergus. 'Thank you,' she added, and then left without another word.

Danny raised his eyebrows and glanced at his grandfather. The first words of praise from Deveraux, however reluctantly spoken, had been a long time in coming.

But Fergus wasn't looking at Danny; he was

deep in thought. They were going overseas in the hunt for Black Star, and that meant a change to his plans for keeping them safe. Fergus was accustomed to having to alter his tactics when an operation took an unexpected turn. This one had; he would turn it to his advantage—but he had to ensure that Danny and Elena were not spooked by the last-minute change.

He knew that Deveraux had gone to send her daily sit rep to Dudley and he waited until Dr Jacobson had left the room too before speaking to the two teenagers. 'Listen,' he said quietly, 'that powder I was telling you about. I'll have to wait until we get to wherever Black Star is taking us before I give it to you.'

'Why?' said Elena. 'What is it, anyway?'

'You don't need to worry about that. I'll get some more in the country we're going to, that's all.'

Danny was getting tired of the way his grandfather was keeping so much information from them. This was the old Fergus, the one he'd first known. 'One minute you're telling us we're a team, and then the next you won't tell us what's going on. We *are* worried—don't you see that?'

Fergus nodded. 'Yeah, course I do. But some things are best kept on a need-to-know basis. If you don't know about it, you can't speak about it.'

'So you don't trust us?'

'You two are the only ones I *do* trust. For now, all you need to know is that the powder I'm going to give to Elena neutralizes the acid in the mix. Which means no big bang. OK?'

Danny realized that he should have known there was always a sound operational reason for his grandfather's decisions. 'Yeah, sorry.'

'No problem.' Fergus smiled at Elena. 'And anyway, like I told you before, we'll get him long before Elena starts mixing up the brew.'

Elena didn't look convinced.

11

Returning to Foxcroft was going to be strange. Spring was moving towards summer, but it felt as though years had passed.

Elena was with Deveraux in the front of the gunmetal-grey Nissan Almera, and Danny was in the back. Deveraux had made it perfectly clear that Danny would be going nowhere near Foxcroft itself, because as far as Dave and Jane Brooker were concerned, he had long since left the area with his grandfather.

But with Fergus booked in for a physiotherapy session on his injured leg back in Oxford, Deveraux had decided that the journey to Camberwell in south-east London, and then on to the Passport Office, located in Eccleston Square, Victoria, would be a good opportunity for her to question the youngsters to see how they were progressing with their training.

A complete cover story had been invented by MI5 to get Elena away from Foxcroft on a temporary basis: Marcie Deveraux was her aunt, her late mother's sister. All the necessary paperwork and documentation had been provided to convince social services that it was quite natural for aunt and niece to spend some time together before deciding whether or not to make the

49

arrangement permanent.

But an unexpected return to Foxcroft was now necessary to collect Elena's birth certificate and to get the application form countersigned by Dave.

Under Deveraux's instruction, Elena had called the Passport Advice Line the previous afternoon to discover the correct procedure for obtaining a passport urgently. She was told she was ineligible for the one-day, Premium Service; that was only available to existing passport holders. The best Elena could get was the Fast Track service, which would guarantee a passport sent to her within a week.

Fergus and Deveraux decided that was the route they had to take. If Black Star were to discover that Elena had been able to find a way around rules and regulations, the entire mission would probably be compromised.

It would have to be a week, and Black Star would have to know why.

The day before, Elena had rung to make an appointment at the office in Eccleston Square, and then they had collected an application form and had some passport photos taken in a booth at Woolworths.

Now, at just before 8:20 a.m., Deveraux parked the car in a side street close to Foxcroft. She had chosen the arrival time deliberately. The young residents of Foxcroft would have left for school by 8:20, which meant that there would be no old friends around for Elena to have 'catch-up' chats with. The fewer people she came into contact with, the better.

Deveraux switched off the engine and turned back to Danny. 'Stay here. We won't be long—I've

50

allowed thirty minutes so that we don't arouse the Brookers' suspicions. So don't you go walkabout. Got that?'

Danny nodded. 'Can you leave the keys in the ignition?'

'Why? Are you thinking of going joyriding?'

'I'm not that stupid,' said Danny with a sigh. 'If I've got to sit here, I might as well listen to the radio.'

Deveraux considered for a moment. 'All right. But not too loudly. I don't want you drawing attention to yourself, or to the vehicle.'

She opened the driver's door and looked at Elena. 'Ready?'

'Yeah. It'll be good to see Dave and Jane.'

'Just be careful what you say,' said Deveraux as she stepped out of the car.

'I *know*!' snapped Elena. 'You've told me a hundred times.' She reached for the door handle and angrily wrenched it open.

'Give my love to Dave and Jane,' called Danny as Elena got out.

Deveraux leaned back into the vehicle and glared at Danny over the back of the driver's seat. 'Don't be stupid.' She moved back and slammed the door just as Elena shut hers.

'Joke!' shouted Danny, watching them walk off down the street. 'Have a nice time.'

He sat back in the seat and waited for a few minutes, watching the pedestrians passing by, half expecting to see someone he knew. Danny had been away from Camberwell for much longer than Elena—over six months. But before that he had lived at Foxcroft for years. If anywhere had ever been home, Foxcroft was as close as it got.

51

Suddenly he wanted to see the old red-brick Victorian building again. He didn't need to go inside—just to see it from the outside would be enough. He knew that Deveraux and Elena would have gone to the front door; he could take a different route to the rear of the building. That was preferable anyway; from across the street he would be able to look up over the back garden wall to glimpse his old bedroom window on the second floor.

He leaned over the driver's seat, pulled the key from the ignition, got out of the car and pushed the door shut. Then he strode off down the street. He had at least twenty minutes to give the old place the once over and be back in time for Elena and Deveraux. Plenty of time.

12

Fergus wasn't with the physiotherapist. One session had been enough to tell him that he could manage the rehabilitation of his damaged body perfectly well for himself. And besides, he had more important things to do.

He was using crutches, for stability and for speed, as he moved down the corridor towards Marcie Deveraux's room at the hotel. He reached the door and gently turned the master key in the lock. One of the first things Fergus had done when they arrived in Oxford was to get hold of a master key and make a copy.

Deveraux's room was the best in the hotel. There was a king-size bed and velvet curtains, and several pairs of expensive shoes were neatly lined up against one wall. A Louis Vuitton suitcase rested on a stand by the window overlooking the garden. Everything was perfectly in place.

Fergus knew exactly where he wanted to go. He rested his crutches against the bed and went directly to the large, dark-wood wardrobe built into a recess opposite the bed. He opened the double doors; there was no need to worry about tell-tales because hotel staff cleaned the room daily. But the safe fixed to the wall at the back of the wardrobe needed to be handled with the utmost care.

The safe was one of the newer types, wide enough to hold a laptop computer. There was an electronic push-button pad for access. Each time the door was opened or closed a four-digit PIN number had to be used. The PIN could be changed as often as required.

Fergus examined the front of the safe within the gloom of the wardrobe, using one of the two small key torches he had on a key ring.

He had been here before and had learned that, exactly as he had expected, Deveraux always put a tell-tale on the safe. Today was no exception. As Fergus checked the front of the safe with the white light from the torch, he saw that one of Deveraux's thick black hairs was stuck across the tiny gap between the door and the safe itself.

It was a tried and trusted method. Deveraux had pulled the hair from her head and then licked it; the spittle providing the adhesive necessary to stick the hair to the metal of the safe. If the door was opened, one half of the hair would break free or it would fall away completely and Deveraux would know that someone had tampered with the safe.

Fergus checked the exact position of the hair and then carefully pulled it free and placed it on a shelf.

He turned on the second small torch. It shone black light, invisible to the naked eye. Fergus had bought the small ultra-violet counterfeit-note detector from a shop in Oxford. And the UV light not only identified counterfeit banknotes and credit cards, it also detected invisible UV ink.

Deveraux's illuminated ink fingerprints were all over the pads of numbers 2,5,7 and 8. They were the numbers she had regularly used when locking or unlocking the safe.

Fergus knew the combination by heart; he had been coming to the room since day one of the operation. The sequence Deveraux used was 8725, but Fergus was always aware that she might have changed it. If that was the case, he would have simply kept hitting different combinations of the four digits until he got it right, just as he had when originally discovering the PIN. It had taken some time to hit on the right number.

But Deveraux had stuck to her usual sequence. The safe's electric lock whirred, the door sprang open and Fergus lifted out Deveraux's neat black laptop.

He smiled as he plugged his iPod cable into the USB port and turned on the laptop to begin downloading the contents of the hard drive. It was no wonder the MoD and large commercial companies had banned iPods from their offices. This was so easy. No hacking into the secure intranet that the security services used on their laptops was necessary to transfer information. The iPod could just bypass it all. Fergus had learned far more than how to download music when Danny had explained the capabilities of the iPod.

The entire download was completed in less than a minute, and Fergus slipped the computer back into the safe, tapped in the PIN and closed the door. He wiped down the keypad with his shirt cuff to remove his own inky fingerprints and then retrieved Deveraux's hair from the shelf. He licked the hair and then stuck it back in its original position. Job done.

Fergus grabbed his crutches, hobbled to the door and listened for any movement in the corridor. There was no sound. Cautiously he left the room, locked the door and then took a small can of UV ink from his pocket. Quickly he sprayed some ink onto the door handle.

He did it daily, always after the chambermaid had cleaned the room. That way, Deveraux always had invisible ink on her hand when she went to the safe. And that way, there were always fresh prints for Fergus to check when he paid his visit.

He headed for his own room. Time to make a coffee and then read the daily sit reps that Deveraux had sent to Dudley.

13

Dave and Jane were delighted to see Elena again, although it didn't take Jane long to remark to Elena that she thought she was looking 'peaky'.

The house was quiet; all the kids had left for school, just as Deveraux had expected. But Jane was full of questions, most of which Deveraux either skilfully deflected or ignored altogether.

Deveraux had an ACA of her own organized. It was a house that she rarely visited, with an impressive-sounding address on the outskirts of Oxford. As far as Dave and Jane were concerned, Elena was living there with her Aunt Marcie.

When Jane asked about schooling, Deveraux explained that she had decided to pay for private tuition for Elena for the time being, rather than enrolling her at a new school. 'Just while we decide on what the future holds for us both,' she said with a convincing smile.

'Oh, but isn't it a bit lonely for you, Elena?' said Jane as she poured herself a second cup of tea from the huge brown teapot that Elena remembered so well. 'Not having any schoolmates around you?' She turned to Deveraux. 'She's always been such a sociable girl.'

Deveraux smiled more broadly than Elena had ever seen her smile before. She knew the smile was false, fake, but then so much about Deveraux was false and fake.

'It's just a temporary thing,' said Deveraux. 'And anyway, Elena and I are spending most of our time getting to know each other.' She looked at Elena, who didn't miss the hint of warning in her eyes. 'Aren't we, Elena?'

Elena's smile was a lot less convincing, but she did her best. 'Mmm.'

'That's why we decided on taking this little holiday together. To get to know each other even better.'

Dave Brooker was leaning against the old range cooker that dominated the kitchen. Both his hands were wrapped around a huge blue and white striped mug. 'Where was it you said you were going?'

'I didn't,' said Deveraux quickly. 'But we're going to Paris and then on to Rome. Rome is so beautiful at this time of year, don't you think?'

Dave took a mouthful of his tea and swallowed noisily. 'Oh, yeah, beautiful,' he said with more than a hint of sarcasm. 'Smashing.'

Dave didn't go in for bullshit, but he saw the look that Jane flashed towards him. He knew it well: it meant 'Behave!' He took another sip of tea and then asked another question. 'What was it you said you do?'

'Do?'

'For a living.'

'Oh, I'm in publishing.'

Dave didn't look impressed, but Jane did. 'How exciting.'

Deveraux shrugged modestly, as if it were no big deal. 'Not really.'

'Have you heard anything from my dad?' said Elena, looking directly at Jane and avoiding Deveraux's stare.

Far more was being said by looks and stares in the Foxcroft kitchen than by words.

'No, darling, I'm afraid we haven't,' said Jane, leaning forward to give Elena a comforting squeeze on the arm. 'Dave and I think he must have gone back to Nigeria. It's a shame for you, I know, but he's probably happier there. And what about Danny—have you heard from him? You two were so close.'

This time Elena did pick up Deveraux's warning look and she shook her head.

'He could be anywhere,' said Dave. 'We haven't

heard a word since he went off with his granddad. What was it, six months ago?'

'Seven,' said Jane. 'We do miss him. I often wonder what he's up to.'

*   *   *

At that moment Danny was standing across the road from the back wall of the Foxcroft garden and staring up at the second floor and his old bedroom window. The curtains were open and he could just glimpse a vividly coloured poster on the bedroom wall. He couldn't see clearly enough to make out what was on the poster, but the colours told him that it wasn't one of his.

He couldn't have expected it to be. Someone had taken over the room that had been Danny's for so many years and made it his own. That was right. Things move on and change, but for Danny the change had been almost total; there was little of his old life to hang on to now.

Only Elena. He forced back the waves of nostalgia and concentrated on the future. Elena had done so much for him and his grandfather over the past seven months. Now it was his turn to do as much for her.

Danny recognized that some of what Elena had written online to Black Star had been for real. Genuine. She was hurting. She hadn't got any family to turn to. It was up to him to look after her.

He took a final look at his old bedroom window and then turned away from Foxcroft and began walking back to the car.

*   *   *

58

Deveraux had decided it was time for her and Elena to make their exit. She finished her tea. 'Well, it's been lovely seeing you both but we need to make our way to the Passport Office. The traffic in Victoria can be awful.' She held the passport application form towards Dave. 'If you wouldn't mind . . . ?'

Dave picked up a pen lying on the kitchen worktop. When he had signed the application form and one of the photographs, Elena stood up, went over to Jane and hugged her.

'Here's your birth certificate,' said Jane, handing it to her. 'Enjoy your holiday. And *please* be careful.' She turned to Deveraux. 'All these terrible bombings going on in the world. You don't know where they'll strike next.'

'I know,' said Deveraux, taking one of Elena's hands in hers. 'But don't worry, I'll look after her.'

They left quickly and Deveraux said nothing more until they were well away from Foxcroft. 'You were supposed to avoid mentioning your father.'

Elena shrugged her shoulders but didn't reply.

They turned a corner into the street where they had parked the car. Up ahead, they could see Danny standing on the pavement.

Deveraux sighed. 'Why do both of you find it so difficult to obey simple orders?'

It wasn't until they got much closer that they spotted the look of panic on Danny's face. Instinctively Deveraux's hand went towards the 9mm Sig pistol that was in the side pocket of her handbag.

But then, as they reached Danny, they saw

exactly why Danny was panicking.

The Nissan. It was gone.

14

Elena was scared. For the first time it looked as though she was really starting to crack under the pressure of the past few weeks. 'Black Star, he's found us.'

'Shut up!' hissed Deveraux. She turned angrily to Danny. 'What happened? Tell me. Quickly!'

Danny knew there was no point in even attempting a lie. 'I just wanted to have a look at Foxcroft. It's been a long time. I was only gone fifteen minutes. Twenty max.'

'And you left the keys in the car?'

'No, I've got them.' Danny held up the key fob. 'Had them with me all the time.'

A blue Vauxhall Corsa slipped into the space until recently occupied by the Nissan. The young driver switched off the engine, got out of the car and pressed his key fob. The Corsa's rear lights flashed, the doors locked and the driver walked away quickly.

Deveraux was still glaring at Danny. 'You did lock the vehicle before you left?'

Danny didn't reply. He didn't need to: the look on his face told its own story.

'Bloody amateurs,' growled Deveraux and glanced at Elena. 'And you! Pull yourself together!'

'Look, I'm sorry,' said Danny quickly. 'I know I messed up—'

'Messed up!' hissed Deveraux. 'You're a disaster.

I should never have agreed to you being part of this operation. I cannot depend on you and that means you put the entire mission at risk. You're out!'

'No!' Elena moved to Danny's side and grabbed his arm. 'If he doesn't go, then I don't! No way! I'm not going without Danny!'

Deveraux said no more. She just punched a number into her Xda to arrange for a replacement vehicle to be delivered to her.

They took a taxi to the Passport Office. Elena was just in time for her appointment, and while she went through the form-filling procedure with an inquisitive official, Deveraux finalized the arrangements for returning to Oxford.

Danny hung around, saying little, looking as guilty as he felt and anticipating the lecture on sticking to SOPs he would no doubt receive from his grandfather when they got back to the hotel.

By early afternoon they were on the M40, heading out of London in a dark blue Vectra. The atmosphere was tense; hardly a word was spoken.

At around 2:30 Deveraux took a call informing her that the Nissan had been found wrapped around a lamppost in Wandsworth.

'Joyriders,' she growled, looking back at Danny.

Danny smiled weakly. 'At least they got it back.'

Deveraux didn't even bother to reply.

15

Pointer kept a silver-framed photograph of his late son Chuck by the side of his computer.

In the head-and-shoulders shot Chuck looked every bit the conventional all-American boy. His body was angled slightly to the right, but his head was turned back towards the camera so that his strong and confident gaze was directed straight at the lens.

His fair hair was parted neatly. His eyes sparkled with humour and good health, and his broad, winning smile was a tribute to the wonders of the dental brace and the expert work of the family's orthodontist.

Chuck looked great. A real picture of health.

Pointer had just pinned another photograph to the wall behind the computer. It was of Elena.

Pointer had had little difficulty in hacking into the UK Passport Service's computer system. It was a relatively simple exploit for a hacker with his skills. As always, he had spoofed his ID and then, with his formidable expertise, had gained root access of the system. Firewalls were no barrier to an expert hacker like Black Star; he had written his own scripts to negotiate his way through or around them.

He found the most recent passport applications and then scrolled through the alphabetical list until he found Elena's, and with it the photograph that had been scanned into the system. All the information was speedily downloaded onto his own computer. Along with the photograph.

It was good for Black Star to study the face of his latest Angel, even though the photograph itself was far less impressive than the one of his son.

Passport photographs rarely did the sitter much justice, and this one was no exception. Elena was staring directly into the camera, her face expressionless, giving little away.

But Black Star felt he already knew everything he needed to know about his latest Angel.

And he knew exactly what to expect the next time he was online with Elena.

I'M SORRY, I HAVE TO WAIT A WEEK TILL MY PASSPORTS DELIVERED.

NO PROBLEM, GOLA. THINGS THIS SIDE TAKE A LITTLE ORGANIZING. BUT EVERYTHING WILL BE READY FOR UR ARRIVAL!!!

'This side!' said Deveraux. 'He's talking about America!'

'Not necessarily,' said Dr Jacobson. 'Could be Europe.'

Deveraux was sitting next to Elena. 'Ask him.'

CAN YOU TELL ME WHERE I'M GOING?

NOT YET, GOLA, BUT I PROMISE U, UR GONNA BE FAMOUS!!!

'Bastard,' breathed Danny.

Elena typed in her next question without waiting for further instructions.

63

WILL I GET TO MEET YOU???

'I didn't tell you to ask him that,' said Deveraux quickly. 'Don't write anything more. And that's an order!'

'I need to know,' said Elena quietly as she stared at the screen.

The operations room was completely silent apart from the slight hum of electricity coming from Elena's laptop. They waited.

WE'LL CERTAINLY MEET UP SOMEDAY, GOLA. NO DOUBT ABOUT THAT.

Elena turned to Danny. 'You're right, he is a bastard.'

YOU STILL FEELING STRONG???

'Tell him you're OK,' said Deveraux.
Elena's hands went back to the keyboard.

FEELING STRONGER EVERY DAY!!!

THAT'S GREAT. B READY 2 LEAVE THE DAY AFTER UR PASSPORT ARRIVES. INFORMATION WILL COME 2 U SOON. AND GOLA, THIS IS IMPORTANT: U MUST TAKE THE HARD DRIVE FROM UR COMPUTER AND DESTROY IT JUST BEFORE U LEAVE. GOT THAT?????

Deveraux nodded to Elena.

YEAH, NO PROBLEM. I'LL DO IT.

64

TERRIFIC. GOTTA GO! B IN TOUCH AGAIN SOON, BYE 4 NOW!!!

16

The training had to continue. With just a week to make final preparations there was still a lot to be covered. Both Fergus and Deveraux knew that much would depend on Danny, wherever the mission eventually took place. And Deveraux had made it perfectly clear to Fergus as the days passed that she was still far from satisfied with his grandson's progress.

Danny's tradecraft skills needed to be sharpened, and Fergus had set him a foot surveillance test. His task was to stake out the Oxford city centre bus station, ping Marcie Deveraux and then follow her as she spent the morning in the city.

Before the exercise began, Fergus took Danny to one side. He wasn't gentle with his last-minute instructions. 'Look, you've fucked up more than once, Danny, and losing the car didn't help. I know you can do the job but Deveraux still wants you out. So don't let me down today, and don't let yourself down. Get out there and show Deveraux she's wrong.'

Danny nodded, but he left for the bus station feeling anxious and uncertain.

For the purpose of the exercise, Deveraux was playing the role of Elena. Danny's job was to follow and watch, because if Deveraux stopped and spoke to anyone and then gave the GO signal, it would mean the person she was with was Black Star.

Danny's first task was to ping Deveraux at the bus station. He sat on a bench by the news stand with a copy of the *Big Issue* in his hands and a pair of earphones in his ears. As always, when on surveillance, he had to appear as natural as possible: he couldn't be seen to be actually looking for someone.

He glanced at the magazine and rocked his head slightly, as if listening to the music coming from his iPod. In reality the machine in his jacket pocket was not even switched on—he had to be completely in tune with the sights and sounds of everything going on around him.

The air brakes of a bus sounded and the doors opened as passengers stepped down from the vehicle. Deveraux wasn't going to make this easy for him, so Danny paid special attention to every black woman he saw. They had done this exercise several times before, and each time Deveraux had changed her appearance as the target. Different clothes, different hairstyle, maybe a hat. And then she would make the follow more difficult by walking slowly, or faster than usual. Sometimes she would stop dead in her tracks and turn round, looking for anything suspicious.

Fergus had told Danny many times that a good ping and pick of the target always led to a good follow. If the ping was messed up, it usually meant that the whole surveillance 'serial' was a series of stumbling cock-ups.

Danny looked over the top of his *Big Issue* and pinged a tall black woman. She hadn't got off one of the arriving buses but had appeared from a side road. She was dressed in jeans, a nylon bomber jacket and a black baseball cap. Her head was down but Danny had followed Deveraux often enough to know her purposeful walk, however much she attempted to disguise it.

He waited for her to pass from left to right before beginning the follow. As Deveraux crossed the busy road and headed for the town centre, Danny was thirty metres behind her. It was the correct distance: any more than thirty metres and he could easily lose her in the crowd; any closer and she might just as easily realize that she was being followed.

Deveraux kept to the right-hand side of the road, so Danny crossed to the left. It was the best position, allowing a little more distance and giving a better view.

It had started well and Danny remembered to keep his eyes down on Deveraux's feet and the blue Nike trainers she was wearing rather than on the back of her head. That way, if she were to turn back suddenly, they were less likely to make accidental eye contact, which would blow the operation.

Danny knew that he had to remain third party aware too. And in these training exercises the third party included his grandfather, who seemed to have a knack for being in the right place when things went wrong for Danny.

Fergus knew the route Deveraux was taking and Danny was only too aware that his grandfather was being driven to different vantage spots so that he could watch his progress.

Deveraux was walking more slowly. Danny did the same—and checked out what was ahead of him so that if she stopped completely, he would have a reason for doing the same. He was in luck: there was a row of shops immediately ahead. Or was it just luck? His grandfather and Deveraux had devised this operation; they would want to see how he reacted to every change in the situation.

As Deveraux came to a halt at a bus shelter, joining two other people, Danny turned and checked out the kettles and radios in the window of a small electrical goods shop. He had his back to the target now, and she was unsighted, so he quickly moved back a little so that the area around the bus shelter was reflected in the window.

The target had been unsighted to him for two or three seconds, long enough to move away. Cars and trucks were passing, and the window Danny was looking into was smeared and grimy. His view was far from perfect but he could just make out the three figures inside the bus shelter. He reckoned that Deveraux's eyes would be burning into his back, just waiting for him to make the error of turning round to check that she was still there.

But Danny knew better than that, and he also knew that he couldn't stand staring at kettles indefinitely. He reached into a pocket of his bomber jacket and took out his mobile phone. It was switched off, but Danny acted as though he was answering a call as he continued to watch Deveraux's reflection in the grimy window.

She must have been satisfied with what he was doing because after another minute she was foxtrot again. After a few seconds, pretending to end the call, Danny was also on the move.

Soon after, Deveraux made another attempt at tricking him. He watched her take a right turn, and instead of following immediately, he walked past the junction and saw that she was still on the right-hand side of the road, passing a row of houses. He turned back and followed, still on the opposite side to Deveraux. She took another right, and Danny immediately became suspicious. Two right turns meant that Deveraux was heading back in the direction she had come from.

As Danny reached the next junction, he saw Deveraux take a third right. He knew exactly what she was doing. She was looping her track, checking to see whether she was being followed. For all Danny knew, she would be round the next corner, with Fergus sitting in a car nearby waiting for him to fall into the trap.

'You don't fool me, Marcie,' whispered Danny as he walked slowly back to the main road. He slipped into a phone box and went through the motions of pretending to make a call while he kept his eyes on the junction where his target was due to appear.

The phone box was good cover from both the third party and the target. When Deveraux appeared—if she appeared—she would see only a shadowy shape there.

Danny waited and began to grow anxious when Deveraux failed to arrive at the junction. Maybe he'd got it wrong; maybe the whole route was anti-surveillance. But his grandfather had told him many times that surveillance was not an exact science. No one could cover all the options. It was a question of weighing up those options and then making a decision. Danny was starting to think he had made the wrong decision, but then Deveraux finally appeared at the junction. He'd got it right.

She crossed the road and headed for the city

centre: Danny said a 'See you then, mate' into the phone, replaced the receiver and started to follow.

In the main shopping area Deveraux lingered to look in a few windows and then Danny saw her check her watch. She started off again, making for a short-term car park. Suddenly she stopped and began speaking to a man heading in the same direction.

Danny went into a bookshop, picked up the first book he saw and, through the shop window, watched the two of them chatting across the street. The man was young; maybe a student. He was wearing trainers, jeans and a blue, chunky pullover.

They spoke for less than a minute and the young man pointed back towards a road in the precinct. Then, as he moved towards an alleyway into the car park, Deveraux took off her jacket.

That was it—the GO sign. As far as the exercise was concerned, Deveraux had been talking to Black Star.

Danny left the shop and headed towards the alleyway, walking swiftly but not running and drawing unwanted attention to himself.

He reached the alleyway and could see the car park at the end. He moved into the gloom of the building, his eyes scanning the immediate area for a glimpse of the blue pullover. He knew that the man was totally unaware that he had become involved in the operation; Deveraux had deliberately selected some unknown third party to give Danny the practice of following a real target.

The young man had disappeared and Danny looked for EXIT signs. He could only see one; about forty metres away to his half left. He made another decision. There was no time to search for

70

Black Star—he might already be driving out of the car park; he might just be walking straight through. But options had to be weighed and decisions made.

Danny walked along to the exit and arrived just in time to see the young man in the blue pullover driving out of the car park in what remained of a rusting green X-reg Mini Metro. As the vehicle stopped at the main road, Danny kept walking, burning the car's registration number into his memory.

The Metro pulled away and disappeared into the traffic. That was it, the serial was over—there was no way Danny could follow Black Star on foot. He powered up his mobile and called Deveraux. She answered after a single ring.

'I've got a vehicle registration and a description for you.'

'End ex. We'll debrief back at the hotel. Now turn round.'

With the mobile still held to his ear, Danny followed the instruction. Deveraux was standing about twenty metres away next to the dark blue Vectra.

Fergus was sitting in the car's front passenger seat.

As Danny powered down his phone, he saw his grandfather's nod of satisfaction. Danny smiled; he'd done it.

17

The information that Black Star had promised arrived in the form of two e-mails, which revealed that Elena would be leaving the UK just three days later. Three days—hardly any time to make preparations, despite all the planning and hurried training that had already taken place.

New York was the destination: Deveraux's hunch had been correct. But there wasn't the time, or even the inclination, to score points in being proved right. There was too much to be done.

The first e-mail was an e-ticket, a return, economy-class flight from Heathrow to JFK, New York. Black Star had thought of everything; a one-way flight would have aroused the suspicions of US immigration officials. But they all knew that the bomb master had no intention of Elena being on board when the return aircraft left the ground.

The second e-mail was a booking confirmation for a two-week stay at New York's Hotel Pennsylvania. Perfect again. The hotel was a popular and affordable destination. Black Star then sent a further e-mail instructing Elena to equip herself with a Lonely Planet guide and a city map and to prepare a cover story.

A girl of seventeen travelling alone was unusual but by no means unheard of. And Elena had watched *Friends* and *Sex and the City* for years, so she almost felt as though she knew the city well enough to get around without a map. All she had to do was make sure she was confident and believable with her cover story. It had to be based on something that was possible, a genuine reason for being in New York.

Deveraux ordered high-speed covert checks to attempt to identify whoever had requested and paid for the airline ticket and hotel reservation. There was a bewildering trail of spoofed IDs through Indonesia into North Africa. Finally it was discovered that both the airline ticket and the hotel room had been ordered and confirmed—but never paid for. A hacker of Black Star's capabilities had no need to pay for anything.

Meanwhile, in a series of meetings with Dudley and high-ranking government officials, Deveraux finalized her immediate plans. But not all those plans were revealed to Danny, Elena or Fergus; yet more secrets in an operation already riddled with secrecy. But that wasn't unusual in the Security Service, where most operations were carried out on a need-to-know basis. It made operational security even tighter.

On the day before departure Deveraux held a last meeting in the operations room at the hotel. Time was short, as she still had to go to London for a final briefing with her boss, Dudley.

'Mission'—Deveraux paused to ensure she had everyone's attention—'to locate and destroy Black Star. Mission—to locate and destroy Black Star.'

Giving the mission statement twice was standard practice; that way everyone understood the exact order. From now on, nothing was more important than the mission, but Fergus knew they were getting only half of the story. No mention had been made of exactly *who* would be doing the destroying. But Fergus was prepared to wait for that information.

73

He, Danny and Elena listened in silence as the operational commander ran through the arrangements for the flights and the arrival in New York and then reiterated procedures for making contact and passing on information once they were on the ground.

Fergus was booked onto an earlier flight than Deveraux, Danny and Elena. He didn't argue with the decision. Travelling with a leg injury such as his brought added complications and he would need extra time to board and leave the plane and to travel to his hotel; he had been booked into the Roosevelt Hotel close to Grand Central Station.

Deveraux pointed at Fergus. 'The reason you are on an earlier flight is to stand by if any immediate help is required by either Danny or Elena when they get to their hotel. You need to be in position before then.'

Fergus nodded. The earlier flight suited him perfectly: it would allow him precious time to finalize some of his own arrangements. Arrangements Deveraux would never know about as they involved their escape route after the job was done.

Danny had been booked into the Pennsylvania, where Elena was staying, but the two friends had to avoid giving any indication that they knew each other. His role was to relay information from Elena once Black Star re-established contact in New York.

'Our plane is due to land at sixteen forty hours,' said Deveraux to Danny and Elena. 'You will carry out a brush contact in the hotel reception area at exactly nineteen forty. You must both adjust your watches by the arrivals display in baggage reclaim.

You should have ample time to clear the airport and check into the hotel. Understood?'

Elena was gazing vacantly through the window towards the garden and the blue, cloudless sky, as she had been for most of the meeting.

'Elena!' said Deveraux sharply.

'Yes, I understand what you want me to do,' said Elena, still looking out at the garden.

Deveraux sighed; there wasn't time for teenage angst. 'The purpose of the contact is for Elena to pass on the location of her chosen DLB and to inform us if Black Star has made initial contact.' She directed her next comment directly at Elena. 'But at no time, Elena, must you prepare anything for Danny while you are inside your hotel room.'

Elena didn't reply, but Danny had worked out why the need for caution was essential. 'You mean Black Star might have set up some sort of bugging or surveillance device in the room?'

'It's highly probable.' Deveraux nodded. 'He's taken the trouble to reserve a room for her.'

Fergus was trying not to show his increasing feelings of concern. 'We have to realize what this guy is capable of at all times. Remember everything I've taught you.'

'That's all I have to say for now,' said Deveraux. 'Questions?'

Fergus shook his head. There were plenty of questions he could have asked. Questions about Danny and Elena's safety. Questions about what exactly would happen when and if they did track down Black Star. But those questions were best left unasked; he had a pretty good idea of what Deveraux was planning at the end of the operation.

Danny, as usual, had no reservations about

asking questions. 'So, we're there to locate Black Star, right?'

Deveraux nodded.

'Well, who does the destroying? You?'

'You concentrate on your part of the mission,' said Deveraux coldly.

Danny sat back in his chair. The answers had been more or less what he had expected, but it had been worth a shot.

'Elena?' said Deveraux.

Elena had gone back to window-gazing.

'Elena!' Deveraux repeated impatiently.

Slowly Elena looked back at her. 'What?' she said quietly.

'Have you any questions?'

'No, I haven't got any questions.'

'I'm surprised. You don't appear to have listened to a word I've said.'

'I *was* listening.'

Deveraux sighed with irritation as she gathered her papers together. 'Very well.' She turned to Fergus. 'We will liaise on my return from London. Now, I have something to do before I leave.'

The meeting broke up and Danny and Elena were left alone after Fergus told them he was going to listen to some music on his iPod.

'You all right?' said Danny, seeing Elena's troubled look.

She shrugged. 'I was thinking about my dad. Wondering when I'll see him again. *If* I'll see him again.'

Danny nodded. 'Are you scared?'

'Of course. Aren't you?'

Danny nodded. 'But my granddad says—'

'Yeah, I know, it's good to be scared. Well, he

76

doesn't look scared. He's always wandering around with that iPod. I didn't even know he liked music.'

'He likes old music. Pink Floyd—something like that. Look, do you wanna watch a DVD? I hate this waiting around—makes me nervous.'

Elena shook her head and stood up. 'No. Sorry, Danny, there's something I want to do too.'

*   *   *

Deveraux was taking personal responsibility for ensuring that Black Star's instruction to destroy the hard drive of Elena's laptop was carried out. She didn't see how he could know whether it had been done or not, but it was best to go along with him at this stage, just in case. Every scrap of information stored in its memory had already been downloaded and forwarded to Security Service experts for further analysis.

She had the hard drive and had taken a hammer from the hotel tool shed. She walked into the garden, dropped the hard drive onto the concrete path and kneeled down with the hammer in her right hand. Three heavy blows were more than adequate to shatter the casing and reduce the copper-plated component board to a twisted, tangled mess.

As Deveraux thumped down on the hard drive for the final time, something made her look up and glance towards Elena's bedroom window.

The teenager was watching her, her face expressionless. Deveraux suddenly felt as though she had been caught in some act of mindless vandalism. Or something far worse—in the act of murder.

She felt exposed and slightly ludicrous, crouched down with the hammer gripped tightly in her hand.

And as Elena stared, Deveraux was unable to stop herself thinking about the night she had killed Joey. It was unfortunate, but Deveraux didn't deal in regrets. There had been no alternative.

The memory of those few moments came back to her: Joey on his knees, his nose pouring with blood while she crouched behind him, both hands around his neck, pulling back the thin edge of her Xda . mobile phone into his crushed windpipe, gradually choking him to death.

As Deveraux shook her head to drive away the vision, she guessed that at that moment Elena was also thinking of Joey. It was almost as if the girl knew what had happened; had somehow worked it all out.

Deveraux looked down at the shattered hard drive and picked it up. She stood up and walked back towards the kitchen door, feeling Elena's eyes burning into her back.

18

Dudley emerged from his meeting with the Foreign Secretary to find Marcie Deveraux waiting for him.

He was his usual business-like self, but the pressure was on for everyone in the Intelligence Services. And the higher up in authority, the higher the levels of pressure. Dudley nodded a brusque acknowledgement to Deveraux, and without a word gestured for her to follow him into a room that had been hastily set aside for their conversation.

It wasn't by any means Deveraux's first visit to the Foreign Office. The main building, with its marble columns, aged colonial oil paintings and heavy chandeliers, always looked to her more like an expensive Parisian hotel than a place of government.

Dudley led the way into one of the wood-panelled reception rooms. The heavy curtains were closed and they sat in armchairs on either side of an ornate low table, where coffee had been set out for their arrival.

The concerned look on Dudley's usually placid-looking face was a sign that his meeting with the Foreign Secretary had not gone completely smoothly.

'Your final arrangements have been made?' he asked brusquely.

'Yes, sir, everything is in place for tomorrow.'

'Good. I don't need to stress the importance of your mission, Marcie. And it is *your* mission.'

There was no need for Dudley to elaborate; Marcie Deveraux fully understood the implications of his words. It was her mission. A deniable mission. She had planned it, the strategy and the tactics.

As soon as it had been established that Black Star was in America, Deveraux was the one who had urged that the mission should remain deniable and that no MoU between the UK and the USA should be arranged. She argued that to share the information with American colleagues would delay the mission. The Americans would throw the full weight of their resources into the operation, quite possibly tipping off Black Star that they were on to him in the process.

Better to keep it small, said Deveraux, compact, the fewer involved the better. Get in, get the job done, and get out. That was the way she operated; it had worked for her in the past and it would work for her this time. Dudley had considered her plan and had then given the go-ahead.

If it was a success, the personal rewards for Deveraux would be enormous. Promotion certainly, and perhaps even Dudley's job. It was well known that he was to retire soon.

On the other hand, failure was too terrible to contemplate. The Americans would go ballistic if they discovered the Brits were conducting a covert operation in New York, involving a planted Angel, and PE with the potential to kill hundreds of US citizens.

Deveraux would be fully responsible and no one else. The Americans would be told that she was a rogue operator who had never been sanctioned to conduct an operation on US soil. She would be thrown out of the Security Service to ensure that good, if damaged, relations were maintained with the US.

Deveraux needed no reminding. She couldn't concern herself with the consequences of failure. She just had to concentrate on the job.

Her cover story was that she was working as a diplomatic attaché at the UN. It meant she would be travelling to and operating in the USA with the comforting security blanket of a diplomatic passport. At any time she could simply claim diplomatic immunity and fly out of the country. If the mission failed, she would be able to return to the UK, but she knew that returning home would not ultimately save her.

No one else involved in the operation had the same level of protection, and that was something Deveraux still needed to discuss with her boss. 'Watts spent years working as a K, sir, which means he's fully aware of what could happen to Danny and Elena. And to himself, of course.'

Dudley nodded. 'Yes. And I'm fully aware of your recommendations with regard to Watts and the teenagers if'—he paused to correct himself—'*when* the mission is successfully concluded.'

'Yes, sir,' said Deveraux. 'I've always believed that they can only be considered a threat to our security. As outsiders, they know far too much and we can never guarantee they will keep silent. As for Watts himself, there's too much history. And I've decided it's too risky to have him in New York. I've made arrangements to deal with that . . . In any event, after the successful conclusion of the mission my recommendation remains the same. They should all be eliminated. We need to clean house after this one, sir.'

Dudley sighed. 'I'm afraid I'm getting too old for this. I shall be glad to get to Dorset, and my bees.' He nodded again. 'It's unfortunate, Marcie, but yes, I agree. Elimination.'

19

Fergus was due to depart from Heathrow two hours before the others. He had kept his farewells to Danny and Elena brief when leaving Oxford, giving them a final reminder to 'take care'.

He had made other arrangements the previous

evening while Deveraux was in London. He had phoned for the DHL parcel delivery company to come and collect a small envelope addressed to Frank Wilson—an alias he had used before, and the one Deveraux had agreed to for this mission—for collection at his hotel, the Roosevelt, which was just a few blocks away from the Pennsylvania.

Inside the envelope were three alias passports, complete with US visa waiver stubs, for himself, Danny and Elena; Fergus had made good use of his old contacts during the weeks in Oxford.

Terminal Four was as busy as ever. Fergus checked in and then joined one of the long lines of passengers waiting to pass through the security checks before going into the departure lounge.

Like most of the other passengers, he took off his jacket and made sure there was nothing metallic in his trouser pockets that would be likely to set off the metal detector as he walked through. He reached the front of the queue, put his jacket in one of the plastic trays and then slid that and the small rucksack he had with him onto the rubber conveyor belt and watched them disappear into the darkness.

He stepped through the metal detector and was relieved not to hear the alert ping, which would have meant an irritating body search. Fergus went to the conveyor belt, put on his jacket and picked up the rucksack. He reached passport control, which had been hastily put in place after the London Underground bombing of 7/7, and showed his passport and boarding card to the waiting security officer.

As he turned to walk towards the departure lounge, he saw two smartly suited men approaching him. He knew instantly who they were: Special Branch. There was no point in panicking; it would have been pointless.

Fergus realized at that moment that he had been set up.

The closest man smiled politely. 'Hello, sir. Can we see your passport and boarding card, please?'

Fergus's passport was in the name of Frank Wilson. The name made no difference: the Special Branch men knew exactly who they were dealing with.

Fergus handed over the passport and boarding card, going along with what he knew was an inevitable process.

The man looked at the passport as he and his colleague escorted Fergus away from the crowds by the security gates. It was a standard practice: move the suspect away from any public areas.

'Just routine, sir,' said the second man as they led Fergus along a corridor and into an office.

It was a small room, the only furniture a desk and a couple of upright chairs. There was hardly enough space for the two Special Branch men, Fergus and the two burly uniformed Metropolitan Police officers, both complete with body armour and MP5 sub-machine guns. One of these was pointing directly at Fergus's head.

Fergus knew the drill. Without even bothering to attempt to protest, he slowly placed his rucksack on the floor, turned round, extended both his arms behind him and waited for the handcuffs to snap into place.

20

Danny was close to the back of the plane, and as the huge Boeing 747 lumbered down the runway, lifted its nose and began its steady climb into the sky, he thought of the last time he had been inside an aircraft.

The two flights could hardly have been more different. This time he was sitting at one end of the central section and was one of several hundred passengers. And even in economy class there was relative comfort and adequate legroom.

On the previous occasion he had been squeezed into the back of a single-engine Cessna alongside his grandfather as they returned to England after six months on the run in Spain.

The tiny plane had collected them, in the dead of night, from an improvised LS deep in the Andalusian countryside, and the highly skilled pilot had used NVGs to negotiate his way through the darkness and onto the ground. They took off knowing only that they were flying into the unknown, as the final struggle to clear Fergus of the accusations laid against him began.

Danny almost smiled as the 747's four huge engines roared and the Jumbo climbed up through the clouds. There was one similarity between the two flights: he was once again flying into the unknown.

But Danny's smile hid the sense of unease he was feeling. Not about the mission—he was feeling good about that, glad that he was part of a crucially important operation of worldwide significance.

He knew that many of his fellow passengers would be thinking about the teenage suicide bombers. Some would be anxious—Danny had noticed the elderly woman next to him give him a long, questioning look as they fastened their seat belts. He had been expecting that sort of reaction; people were bound to be unnerved by the sight of a teenager travelling alone. But Deveraux and his grandfather had briefed him well, and Danny had eased the woman's fears with a smile and a few well-chosen words about the long flight ahead.

He had also dealt skilfully with the extra-long questioning and the bag and body search he had been subjected to when going through security to the departure lounge at Heathrow.

Danny glanced across to his right and saw the newspaper headline:

HUNT FOR BOMB MASTER

Little did the passenger reading the newspaper know that someone at the forefront of that hunt was sitting just a few seats away.

And despite his grandfather's fears over Deveraux, Danny felt excited about whatever lay ahead. But there was a nagging worry: Elena.

After their short conversation at the end of Deveraux's briefing the previous afternoon, Danny had seen no more of Elena until this morning. She had stayed in her room all evening, not even bothering to come down for dinner.

She had reappeared at breakfast but had been quiet and withdrawn, even when Fergus had said his farewells.

And then, just as they were about to say their

85

own awkward goodbyes, Elena had done something that seemed to surprise them both. She had kissed Danny; fleetingly brushing her lips against his before whispering, 'Goodbye, Danny.'

Before a stunned Danny could even reply, she was gone, apparently not wanting to prolong the parting any more than was absolutely necessary. Danny didn't like the word 'goodbye' when it came from Elena. He was used to 'see ya' or 'later', or even 'bye', but 'goodbye' was weird. Too . . . final.

They travelled separately to Heathrow— Deveraux had insisted on that, just in case Black Star, or an associate, was watching out for Elena on this side of the Atlantic. It was unlikely, but Deveraux was taking no chances.

As Danny unbuckled his seat belt and made himself more comfortable, he was thinking about the way things had been not quite right between him and Elena over the past few weeks. There was a strange distance between them that had never been there before. He told himself that it was his fault. He had been so wrapped up in the mission that he had neglected Elena's feelings at the time when she needed him most. And he felt bad about it. And worried. And guilty.

*   *   *

Elena was sitting in a window seat, a little closer to the front of the plane. Next to her was a huge middle-aged American woman, who had started to chat even before her more than ample backside hit the seat.

By the time the engines had begun their starting whine, Elena knew that her travelling companion was called Mavis Bachelor and that she was married to Henry—whom 'just everyone called Hal'—and that Hal was in the meat-packing business.

'You look a little scared, honey,' said Mavis as they picked up speed. 'There really is no problem with flying. You have more to worry about when you cross the road.'

But Elena wasn't worried about the flight. That was the least of her worries.

*   *   *

Marcie Deveraux was at the front of the plane, in first class. The businessman sitting next to her had done no more than nod a polite 'Hello' as he took his seat. She had nodded back in the same way, relieved that he obviously had no intention of passing the flying hours attempting to make meaningful, interesting conversation.

He was already working at his laptop as Deveraux sat looking at the menu for the first of the meals they would be served during the eight-hour flight.

Her eyes flicked over the menu and she allowed herself a slight smile as she considered what Fergus Watts might have to look forward to for his next meal. By now he would be in a cell and would have realized that she had arranged for him to be lifted at the airport.

He would remain in a cell until Deveraux returned at the end of the mission. And then, along with Danny and Elena, he would be eliminated.

Deveraux had never intended Fergus to be part of the final phase of the operation, and the fact that it was overseas had made it easier for her. His participation in phase one had been essential: Danny and Elena would never have agreed to being involved, had Fergus been jettisoned at that stage. And he had been more than useful in their training—Deveraux silently acknowledged that she wouldn't have been able to move them on so quickly or efficiently.

But now he was unnecessary; his presence in New York would have been a liability and there would undoubtedly have been problems when it came to making decisions that might put Danny or Elena in danger.

There would still be problems when Deveraux had to explain to the teenagers why Fergus was not with them in New York.

But she would cope with that. She had it all worked out.

*   *   *

Herman Ramirez was weary; the past few months had been exhausting with the intercontinental flights and the subsequent jet lag. But Herman never complained and this time it would be easier. This time the Angel was flying to them.

Herman was good with electronics, and there were certain electronic adjustments he needed to make to Elena's room at the Hotel Pennsylvania before her arrival.

He worked methodically and with total concentration. Herman did things right.

A pencil-sized camera had been fitted into the TV, enabling it to draw power from the set at all times. It was located behind a small hole in the speaker. The mic had been placed in the ceiling light and was also drawing constant power.

Both devices would radiate their weak signals via the power cables by which they were fed to a rebroadcaster. The suitcase-sized device was located in a Winnebago, which Herman had earlier left in a long-term parking lot one block from the hotel.

The rebroadcaster's function was to pick up and encrypt the weak signals from both camera and mic and then boost the power before relaying the signal on its onward journey towards Pointer's home in The Hamptons.

There, the encrypted signal would eventually be decoded and Pointer's monitor and speaker would relay what was taking place in the room approximately two seconds after it had happened.

Herman completed his work, packed away his tools, checked his watch and slipped from the room as noiselessly as he had entered it.

*　　　*　　　*

Before take-off Elena had feared her arrival in New York and what it would bring. But when she heard the announcement that the aircraft was beginning its descent, she felt relieved.

Mavis was a talker. Elena now knew the entire Bachelor family history. The only time Mavis didn't talk was when she was eating, and then only when she was actually chewing and swallowing. Between mouthfuls she picked up wherever she had left off.

Short of being rude and telling her to shut up, Elena had tried everything to get a break from the verbal onslaught. She read, she stared out of the window, she watched movies, but Mavis just kept on talking.

There had been a brief respite of a couple of hours when Mavis had dropped off to sleep. Elena gratefully did likewise, but her dreams were dark and disturbing and she was almost relieved when her neighbour's piercing voice brought her back to consciousness. The only good thing about Mavis's chatter was that she didn't ask questions; she was far too busy talking about herself.

The aircraft slipped lower and followed the coastline over The Hamptons. Mavis was gathering her things together. 'Hal will be waiting for me; he'll be just *dying* to tell me everything that's happened while I've been away. He really is the most wonderful husband but he never stops talking. Once he gets going, I just can't get a word in.'

She delved into her huge handbag, pulled out a business card and pressed it into Elena's hands. 'It's been just wonderful chatting to you, Elena, you're such an interesting girl. Now, you make sure you come and visit the Bachelors of Brooklyn Heights if you get a moment. The phone number and address are on the card. Just call, any time.'

Elena smiled and slipped the card into her jacket pocket. 'That would be great. Thanks very much.'

21

Touchdown was as smooth as the flight itself had been. During the journey Elena had only glimpsed Danny a couple of times as she made her way to the toilet at the back of the plane. But they hadn't even exchanged a glance; they couldn't afford to.

Deveraux had ordered a check on every passenger on the flight. It had revealed nothing, but she knew perfectly well that Black Star could be among the hundreds of people on board that aircraft.

Elena didn't see Danny as she left the 747. Clutching her completed green visa waiver and white customs forms, she walked into the new glass-and-steel terminal building and joined the long, snaking immigration queue. She spotted Danny further back down the line and then caught a glimpse of Marcie Deveraux as she made for the diplomats' section and walked straight through without a glance in their direction.

Elena finally reached the front of the queue. She stepped forward and handed over her passport and forms to the uniformed immigration officer, who studied them all thoroughly.

She waited nervously until the officer looked up. 'How long are you staying?'

'Two weeks.'

'And you're here alone? Your parents are OK with that?'

'I don't have parents,' said Elena quickly. 'Not any more. When my mum died she left me some money for travelling. Wanted me to see more of the world than she ever did. New York seemed the best place to start because I've seen so much of it on TV and I love it. So here I am.'

'You're pretty young to be travelling alone.'

Elena nodded and then pulled out the card that was in her pocket. 'But I won't be alone all the time. I've got American friends—Mavis and Hal Bachelor. Actually, they were friends of my mum.

They live in Brooklyn Heights and they've promised to show me the sights.'

'But you're not staying with them?' said the officer as he looked at the card.

Elena smiled. 'They're a lot older than me. We thought it was best if I stayed at the hotel. That way we can see each other as much as we want, but probably not every day.' She waited, expecting her questioner to say something. He didn't, so Elena smiled again. 'Look, I'm seventeen. They'll treat me like a child.'

The officer considered for a moment longer and then handed the card back. 'Can I see your return ticket, please?'

Elena handed over the ticket, and the officer took in the details and then passed it back. He tore off the bottom part of the green visa waiver form and stapled it to Elena's passport. Then he put a small cross on the bottom of the customs form and gave the passport back to Elena.

Attached to the counter between them was a small rectangular metal box with a yellow light shining from its glass top. The officer nodded towards the box. 'Place your right index finger over the light, please.'

Elena did as she was instructed and her fingerprint was captured. The process was repeated with her left index finger and then the officer reached up and shifted an oval camera fixed to an adjustable arm so that it was at the same level as Elena's head.

'Look at the camera, please.'

The camera clicked and the officer smiled for the first time. 'Enjoy your stay, and take care.'

As Elena made her way to baggage reclaim, she

could feel her heart pumping, but she was pleased with herself for getting through immigration, with the help of Mavis and Hal Bachelor. It would be a lot easier now; soon she would be on her way to the hotel.

She looked up at the plasma screen displaying the arrivals' flight numbers and checked for the carousel where her suitcase would eventually arrive. While she waited, there was a job to be done. The time on the bottom right-hand corner of the arrivals screen read 5:27 p.m. Deveraux had briefed them in advance, so she knew that the majority of clocks in the US would use a.m. and p.m. rather than the twenty-four-hour system. Elena pulled out the winder on her wristwatch and set it for 5:28 p.m. She waited until the arrivals display changed and then pushed in her winder.

Suitcases of every size, make and colour went trundling by. Once Elena glimpsed Danny on the far side, and for just a second their eyes met. Elena hoped briefly for at least a smile of encouragement but Danny quickly looked away.

He was sticking to orders and Elena found herself wondering if and when they would actually speak again. Suddenly there were so many things she wished she had said to Danny before they left England. But it was too late now.

Her bag finally appeared and she heaved it off the carousel and walked through to another queue at customs.

The questioning was far from over.

As soon as the waiting officer spotted the cross on the bottom of the customs form, he gestured for Elena to follow him to a desk and asked her to open her suitcase. A female officer, wearing a pistol on her hip, joined them and began a thorough search of both the suitcase and the small shoulder bag Elena had with her.

And while she searched, the other officer repeated many of the questions Elena had already answered. And a few more. 'Your address in England?'

Elena gave her ACA, the hotel in Oxfordshire. 'I work there,' she said.

'And the phone number?'

She told him the number.

'What's that number again?'

Elena repeated the number, but faster, realizing exactly what was happening. Fergus had warned them that they might well be tested on both address and phone number and had quizzed them himself repeatedly during the training period. Remembering them was second nature now.

The female officer pulled some small rectangles of Velcro from Elena's suitcase and held them up. 'What are these for?'

'My bum bag.'

Both officers stared. 'Your *what*?' said the woman.

'You know, bum bag. I'm gonna buy one here to keep my cash in and I brought the Velcro to make it more secure.'

The officers exchanged a look. 'She means a fanny pouch,' said the man.

'Do I?' said Elena.

The female officer smiled, slid the Velcro back into the suitcase and put Elena's Lonely Planet guide and city map back into her shoulder bag. 'What do you plan on seeing?'

'The Empire State Building, and the Statue of

94

Liberty, of course,' said Elena confidently. 'But I really want to go to Ground Zero. I watched it on TV; it was terrible. I just feel I ought to go—I think everyone should.'

The officer sighed as she completed her search. 'I hear you. Me and my sister went just last month. Don't know why, just kinda felt we had to.' She nodded to her colleague.

It was over at last. Elena zipped up her suitcase and walked through to the arrivals hall.

Marcie Deveraux would have already left the airport and was being driven to her hotel in a prearranged limo. Danny was taking a taxi.

Elena followed the signs for the shuttle bus that would take her into the city. She was tired; her heavy bag banged against her legs with each weary step. And as she walked towards the bus, the thought crossed her mind that perhaps Black Star might be somewhere in the crowd.

No one approached her; Black Star was not there.

But other eyes had locked onto Elena, and if she had looked closely she might have recognized the faces of Deveraux's operatives Fran and Mick.

Posing as a newlywed couple on honeymoon, they had arrived in New York the previous afternoon. Now they mingled with the crowd and watched.

And theirs were not the only eyes watching her.

Herman Ramirez was standing among the cab drivers and chauffeurs waiting for those passengers who had booked rides into the city. He nodded with satisfaction as he got his first look at Elena. He could now report to his master: the Angel had landed.

22

The fifty-minute ride on the shuttle bus from the airport into the heart of the city should have been an incredible experience for a young first-time visitor to New York.

The differences between London and New York were remarkable and amazing. The roads, the lines of streaming traffic, but mostly, as Elena caught her first glimpse of the Manhattan skyline, the size and scale of the soaring buildings, reaching upwards like the fingers of dozens of upturned hands.

But the whole wonderful, frenetic scene passed Elena by. A great lump of anxiety in her chest seemed to swell with every passing mile, making it difficult to breathe properly. Each breath was snatched and shallow as her unease grew. Black Star was out there somewhere. Waiting.

It was almost seven o'clock—midnight back home in England—when Elena finally got off the bus and walked the short distance, past Madison Square Garden, to the Hotel Pennsylvania. In the hotel's small coffee shop just inside the revolving doors, Danny was sitting at one of the tables. He saw Elena go by, but he didn't move. He had checked in earlier, and all he needed to know for now was that Elena had arrived safely. He pulled out his secure mobile phone to call Deveraux and his grandfather. Everyone was on the ground and the operation was about to kick off.

The lobby and reception area was busy and bustling with new arrivals waiting to check in.

Elena joined yet another queue.

She looked around as she waited. The entrance to the lifts was behind her. A couple of security men were standing by to check that only those with key cards actually made it through to that area. Most people were minding their own business, talking on mobiles, studying city guides or maps, or heading for the bar or the coffee shop. No one appeared to be taking any particular interest in Elena, but she knew that didn't mean no one was watching.

'Can I help you?'

Elena was looking towards the bar, where a young Chinese guy dressed in jeans, T-shirt and a thin, unzipped bomber jacket seemed suddenly to be paying her special attention. He was staring directly at her. She felt her heart thud in her chest, but then he turned his head slightly and Elena saw that his lips were moving. She could just see the earpiece in his right ear. He was talking hands-free on his mobile, far more interested in his conversation than in anything in his eye-line.

'Excuse me, miss, can I help you?'

The voice was a little louder and more insistent, and Elena turned her head to see a man behind the reception desk smiling patiently in her direction. She had reached the front of the queue without even realizing it.

'Sorry, I've got a room booked.'

'Sure. And your name, please?'

'Elena Omolodon.'

The clerk frowned slightly. 'Can you spell that for me?'

Elena spelled out her name quickly, each letter making her more acutely aware of the vulnerability

97

of her position; she didn't even have the protection of a cover identity.

The check-in clerk scrolled down his computer screen and found the reservation Black Star had made online. It was perfectly in order, and as far as the clerk was concerned, everything had been correctly booked and paid for in advance.

He smiled. 'Could I see your passport, please?'

Elena handed over the brand new passport and the clerk tapped a few details into his computer before giving it back, along with a thin sliver of credit-card-like plastic, which was the key card to Elena's room.

'The account's been taken care of. You're on the eighth floor—elevators are right over there,' said the clerk, pointing straight ahead. 'Welcome to New York.'

Elena smiled a thanks and picked up her suitcase, but as she turned away, the clerk spoke again. 'Just one moment, please.'

'What's wrong?' said Elena, fearing that she had made some sort of mistake.

'Nothing at all wrong, miss. I just have a note here that we have something for you.'

'For me?'

The clerk nodded, reached beneath the desk and took out a heavily taped padded envelope. 'This was left for you earlier today.'

'For me? Who left it?'

'No idea, miss. It was before I came on duty.'

Elena took the envelope and saw her name in large type on the front. She shivered. It was from him. Black Star. It had to be. She grabbed her suitcase again and walked over to the lifts, joining the others waiting to go up. No one spoke and no one looked at anyone else as they rose quickly from floor to floor: seven people in a confined space acting as though they were alone. With just their luggage and their thoughts.

Elena was the only person to get out on the eighth floor. She stepped out into the corridor and saw the sign indicating the direction of her room. She went along the corridor, and found her room, then noticed, further along, a double door with a window in it. Through the glass in the doors Elena could see a drinks dispensing machine and another loaded with different sweets and chocolate bars. Opposite them was an ice machine. Perfect.

She dumped her suitcase in the corridor and pushed through the doors. She went over to the drinks dispenser, looked at it for a few moments and then moved to the back of the machine and peered behind it. She sorted through the change she'd got from the bus ride, found some quarters and got a can of Fanta from the machine. Then she turned away, went back into the corridor and picked up her suitcase.

Elena returned to her room, slid the key card into the slot and heard the lock click open. Wearily she pushed open the door, flicked on the lights, heaved her suitcase into the room and dumped it on her bed.

Two seconds later Charles Pointer II got his first onscreen look at his new Angel.

*　　*　　*

It was 1:30 a.m. in Oxford and Dr Ruth Jacobson was sitting on the bed in Elena's old bedroom.

Hotel cleaning staff had already cleared the

room of most of the things Elena had left behind; it was almost as though she had never been there. Only one item remained—her laptop.

Dr Jacobson was staring at the machine, which sat on top of a small writing desk. She should probably leave it at reception for Elena to collect on her return from America.

Dr Jacobson had spent the day at the hotel, finishing up, writing her final report for Marcie Deveraux. She decided there was nothing more for her to do, and tomorrow she would move on to another case: someone else's story, someone else's problems. But this process had to be gone through at the end of every assignment and sometimes she was far more satisfied with her work than others.

She couldn't help feeling that she had failed in her work with Elena. The girl had held up well to begin with, but by the time she left for New York she had been showing signs of anxiety and stress. She had lost weight, and had looked drawn with fatigue. Dr Jacobson's chief concern, which had been mostly ignored by Deveraux, was that Elena's state of mind was likely to get worse when she was working alone, isolated from her friends and any professional support.

The only light in the room came from the desktop lamp, which shed most of its light downwards, picking out and spotlighting the laptop computer like an item of scenery on an open stage.

Dr Jacobson finished her notes; there was nothing more to be done. Time to go. She got up from the bed and walked over to the desk. She reached down and picked up the laptop; as she did so, she saw a white envelope, folded in the middle, slip from underneath the machine. She turned over the computer and saw that the battery had been removed; the envelope had been nestling inside the empty compartment.

She put down the laptop, looked at the sealed envelope and unfolded it, so that the front was exposed. Written in black ink and capital letters was a single word:

DAD

23

Elena sat on the end of her hotel bed with the padded envelope in her hands. She was annoyed to see that her fingers were trembling as she twisted and snapped the tape securing the package. She pulled away the last of the tape, opened the top of the envelope and peered inside. Something small was enclosed in bubble wrap, and next to that was a thick wad of US banknotes. As she pulled them out of the envelope, she found a single sheet of paper taped to the bubble wrap, neatly folded twice so that it was almost exactly the same size as the package itself.

She dropped the dollars onto the bed, unfolded the sheet of paper and read:

`Turn on the power.`

The paper joined the banknotes on the bed as Elena began to open the bubble wrap, already guessing what was inside. She almost smiled as the brand new BlackBerry device was revealed. As usual, Black Star had thought of everything.

Without even removing her jacket, Elena sat down and powered up the BlackBerry. It opened straight onto a secure personal site in her name on a website she had often used in the past.

In his darkened room in The Hamptons, Pointer smiled as he watched Elena's face.

'Time to talk,' he whispered, his fingers moving across to his computer's keyboard.

Hi Gola, glad u made it ok. Thought this woz best way 4 us 2 b in contact now ur here. So how ya doin??? Room ok???

Elena almost dropped the BlackBerry. It was like he was there, inside the room with her, rather than just sending her an IM. She hesitated, uncertain how she should reply: she realized that this was the first time since the operation had begun that she had been completely alone when in contact with Black Star. Where she would normally have looked to Deveraux or Dr Jacobson for an instruction, now she had no one. She was really on her own with this thing, and if the operation was to succeed, she had to get it right. So many people were relying on her. She shivered. She was so tired. Her brain didn't feel capable of logical thought. And yet the one thing she knew she felt comfortable with was technology. A BlackBerry? A breeze! She took a deep breath, thought for a moment and then her thumbs began to move over the keypad.

Im ok, bit tired, long day. Is this safe?? Secure?

The reply came straight back.

Hey, Gola, u may b tired, but ur still thinking good. Normally it might not b safe, but 4 us its perfectly secure. We're just hitchin a ride on this site, they dont even know we're here. And they never will!!!!

Elena couldn't help but marvel at the hacker's incredible ability to go wherever he desired on the Internet without leaving a single trace. But before she could comment, Black Star came back.

So heres wots goin down tonite. First, I need you 2 tear that sheet of paper in2 small pieces and flush it down the toilet. Do it now!!!

Suddenly Elena knew for certain that somehow Black Star was watching her. She found herself glancing around the room, not knowing what she was looking for, only that somewhere there was a camera.

Do it, Gola, we have 2 stay safe!!!

Elena rested the BlackBerry on the bed and grabbed the sheet of paper. She was already ripping it to shreds as she walked into the bathroom. The pieces fluttered down into the lavatory bowl and Elena flushed them away. As she waited for the swirling water to calm, she had a sudden, cold thought. If Black Star was watching her in the bedroom, could he be watching her here too?

She went back into the bedroom and picked up the BlackBerry.

Done.

Great! Ya done good. Now, Im gonna tell you about ur cool nite out!!!

For a moment Elena felt herself panic. She hadn't expected to be going out that evening and she knew she still had to establish a DLB and then carry out a brush contact with Danny to pass on the details in just twenty minutes' time.

Nite out???

Sure, Gola, I want 2 give u the perfect example of exactly y we're doin wot we're doin. Show u the sort of people who run this world and dont give a shit about people like us!!! U up 4 it????

*   *   *

Danny checked his watch for the tenth time since arriving in his room on the eleventh floor of the Pennsylvania. It was time to move.

But there was a problem. Danny still hadn't made contact with his grandfather. He had checked in with Deveraux first, exactly as ordered, but since then he had been calling Fergus's mobile every few minutes and had got the voicemail every time.

He decided to give it one more go but the same thing happened. Danny didn't like it; it didn't feel right for the beginning of the operation to be rough at the edges. Maybe Fergus wasn't answering for the simple reason that the battery in his phone wasn't keeping its charge. But it wasn't like Fergus to let a situation like that persist; he'd just go out and get another phone.

Danny called Deveraux again. 'Look, I know I'm not meant to contact you again now, but I've been trying to get my granddad for ages and I can't. I'm worried.'

Deveraux's response was cool and unruffled. 'There's been a problem; he was lifted at Heathrow. We're doing everything we can to get him released and out here as planned.'

Danny was stunned into silence for a few moments, although his mind was racing as he attempted to figure out whether or not Deveraux was giving him the true story. He doubted it, but right then, there seemed little he could do. 'So who lifted him, and why?'

'He is still officially a wanted man, Danny—'

'But I thought his name had been cleared—'

'Yes, well . . . it all takes time. It was Special Branch, simply doing their job. As far as they're concerned, he's still on the wanted list. While we attempt to get him out, *our* job is to get on with what we're here for, which means sticking to SOPs. Your grandfather would tell you that himself.'

That much was true enough—Fergus would certainly have told Danny to stick to SOPs—but Danny wasn't naive enough to believe Deveraux was giving him the whole picture. It was just too convenient. Fergus didn't trust Deveraux and Danny didn't either. But there was still the mission, and Elena, to think of.

Danny suddenly realized that if Fergus never

105

made it out to New York, he would have to take on the responsibility of ensuring that he and Elena got out, once the mission was completed. But how could he do that? His grandfather had been taking care of all the arrangements. 'OK,' he said. 'But you'll let me know as soon as you hear anything?'

'Yes. But don't tell Elena about this in any DLB messages. She has a job to do, and with or without your grandfather, the mission goes ahead as planned.'

'Yeah, all right.'

'And Danny, I repeat, stick to SOPs—no Fergus Watts-style heroics.'

Deveraux ended the call and Danny sat back on his bed, trying to weigh up what he needed to do in his grandfather's absence, and he realized immediately that there was another thing he couldn't do: he couldn't provide the powder that made mix thirty-nine safe. Fergus was meant to get it in New York, and Danny didn't even know what it was. He just had to hope that Elena would never have to make the PE.

The plan for the scheduled brush contact was that Danny would leave the hotel, go and buy a city guide and then be back in reception exactly on time. He and Elena would carry out the brush contact as she walked away from the lifts and he walked towards them. Simple, but as they both knew, simplicity didn't always mean success.

Danny left his room, took the lift down to reception, walked out through the revolving doors, turned to his left and strode purposefully away down the street. Fifteen minutes to go. He knew that for now, despite his worries about Fergus, he had to remain focused on the job in hand.

It was still light, but up above the towering buildings the sky was heavy with darkening clouds that threatened a downpour before the night was through. The pavements were heaving with bodies, the traffic was nose to tail, and everywhere was noise and movement.

Danny was overawed by the size and spectacle of Manhattan. It was just like the movies. Only bigger. To his right was Madison Square Garden. Danny's sport was athletics; he had run long-distance and cross-country for his county. He had no particular interest in boxing, but even he knew that many of the greatest fights in the history of the sport had taken place in that arena.

Danny kept walking for five minutes, passing at least one store where he could have stopped to buy a guide, but he was using up time, taking in the sights like any normal tourist. Always have a reason for doing whatever you are doing; it was one of the golden rules, an SOP.

Danny smiled as he passed a metal grille in the roadway where steam poured up from somewhere below. Just like the movies. He checked his watch again as he reached another store: nine minutes to go. He went inside, plucked a city guide from a revolving stand and went up to the counter to pay.

He was back outside and retracing his steps with seven minutes to go. Four and a half minutes later he was staring at the front of the hotel. His natural impulse to be there on time had caused him to walk a little quicker than before. He stopped, took the guide from his jacket pocket and opened it, staring at a page as though he was refreshing his memory on some city site of special interest.

He looked at his watch again, knowing that this

107

must be the final time. Anyone seeing him checking his watch every thirty seconds or so might become suspicious.

Danny slipped the guide back into his pocket and went back into the hotel reception with less than a minute to go. It was still busy, with new arrivals at the desk and others going to and from the coffee shop. But as Danny's eyes scanned the area, he quickly realized that Elena was not there.

He went to the reception desk and picked up a couple of leaflets offering guided tours of the city. As he stood and pretended to read, he was counting down the seconds. Elena had still not appeared.

The doors to one of the lifts opened and five people stepped out. But not Elena. She was late: something must have happened to her. Danny's thoughts were racing. He couldn't just stand there indefinitely; he couldn't go up to one of the desk clerks and ask them to call Elena's room; but he had to make a decision.

Danny knew that SOPs demanded that if Elena didn't show, he should go away and return exactly thirty minutes later to try again. But just like not being able to reach his grandfather on the phone, it didn't feel right, not so soon after their arrival.

It was two minutes past contact time and Danny was about to walk back to the coffee shop when another lift arrived at the ground floor and the doors slid open. Elena was there, in a crowd of seven or eight people.

The brush contact was still on; late but still on. Danny dropped the leaflet back onto the desk and turned to walk towards the lift. As he neared Elena, he could just see the small black 35mm film container in her right hand. He thought back to the first time they had attempted this manoeuvre, when the canister had ended up tumbling to the ground. They couldn't afford a repeat of that disaster; they had no idea who might be watching, and there was also the hotel CCTV system. If an alert security guard saw the contact on a monitor screen, it could easily be taken as a drugs deal, and then Danny and Elena would be lifted and the operation would be compromised before it had even started.

The gap between them narrowed to less than two metres; there were just a couple more strides for them both. Danny's right hand was at his side; his fingers opened just enough to receive the canister. They had not once made eye contact.

And then they were side by side, and the canister slipped from Elena's right hand into Danny's. The exchange was as clean and smooth as a perfect baton change by a couple of Olympic sprinters.

Danny could feel the soft part of the Velcro that Elena had stuck all the way around the canister. He kept walking towards the lifts without looking back; he didn't see Elena go through the revolving doors and leave the hotel.

24

In her penthouse suite at the exclusive Four Seasons Hotel on East 57th Street, Marcie Deveraux gazed out through the picture window across the Manhattan skyline as she spoke into her Xda. 'She's going *where*?'

'A Japanese restaurant,' said Danny into his mobile as he re-read the note Elena had slipped into the canister. 'At the Time Warner Center at Columbus Circle. He's made a reservation and she's on her way there now.'

Deveraux had heard of the new, highly acclaimed development on the south-west corner of Central Park, but had not yet visited it. The two massive towers housed expensive office space and a luxury hotel and were connected by a huge glass and steel central area with classy restaurants and shops. 'Give me the name of the restaurant,' said Deveraux into her Xda.

Danny was in his room at the Hotel Pennsylvania. He read out the name written on the paper.

'What else?' snapped Deveraux.

'Elena's sure there must be some sort of surveillance device in the room. She's sure he's watching her somehow.'

'Just as we thought. Continue.'

Danny was desperate for news of his grandfather. 'What about my granddad? What's happened?'

'There's nothing I can tell you at the moment.'

'What? But you must have done something to get him out!'

'It isn't easy, Danny. Your grandfather has been a wanted man for a very long time. Special Branch believe they've made quite a coup in capturing him. We are attempting to persuade them to hand him over to us, without giving details of exactly why we want him.'

'But surely you can—'

'Enough!' said Deveraux. 'Now continue with

your sit rep.'

Danny knew there was no point in pressing Deveraux further; she would say nothing more. He looked at the note Elena had written. 'Black Star has given her a BlackBerry. They're making contact through a website, but Elena says he's told her it's completely secure.'

'Yes, I'm certain it is. What about her DLB? Where is it?'

'Back of the drinks dispenser along the corridor on her floor,' said Danny as he double-checked Elena's instructions. 'And we're using a concrete waste bin outside the hotel as our "DLB live" marker location.'

The sky was darkening and, all over the city, lights were beginning to stud the gloom. 'Good,' said Deveraux as she walked away from the window and sat down on one of the suite's stylish and comfortable sofas.

Fergus had trained them thoroughly in the limited time he had had. A 'DLB live' marker meant that there was something in the Dead Letter Box for collection. Danny and Elena had both brought small adhesive paper dots in their luggage. If either of them had a message to pass on to the other, they would stick one of the dots on the waste bin to show that the DLB was 'live'.

'We need that BlackBerry,' said Deveraux. 'Leave Elena a message for when she gets back tonight. We need to know Black Star's latest orders, and we must have the BlackBerry tomorrow morning, just for a few minutes. Let her know that it will be out of her control for no more than fifteen minutes.'

'But . . . but what happens to the BlackBerry

when I get it? Maybe Black Star will know we have it.'

Deveraux had no intention of wasting her breath giving Danny information he didn't need. 'I want that BlackBerry by o-nine-thirty hours. Elena will leave her room for breakfast long before then. You will decide on the time, method and place for the contact and you will leave Elena the details tonight. I will call you at o-eight-hundred hours with your RV instructions for when you have the BlackBerry. Do you understand?'

'Yeah, but what if—?'

Deveraux's voice rose with irritation. 'Just do as you're ordered, Danny. I don't have time for explanations. And tell Elena to keep the TV set in her room switched on and tuned to the C-SPAN political station when she leaves her room tomorrow. If Black Star asks her why, she is to say it is for security; it sounds as if someone is in the room. Tell her also to put the "Do Not Disturb" sign on the door.'

'Why?'

'Don't question me. Just do it!'

Danny was accustomed now to Deveraux telling him the bare minimum. 'Yeah, right. I'll sort Elena's instructions and then get down to Columbus Circle to see what's happening.'

'You will do *nothing* of the kind! Once you've made the DLB live, your work for tonight is over. You are to go nowhere near the hotel reception or Elena's floor once she returns. Make the DLB live and then keep out of the way. Is that understood!'

'But—'

'Is it *understood*?!'

Danny took a deep breath. Deveraux was in

command of the operation and was giving the orders, but that didn't stop him worrying about Elena.

She was out there alone, and no doubt afraid, and Danny was more conscious than ever of his promise to be there for her. 'I'm just worried about Elena,' he said.

'You're not here to worry, you're here to follow orders.' Deveraux's tone was controlled but menacing as she continued. 'So follow them.'

Orders. Always orders. Sometimes Danny found it so difficult to follow orders, especially when they went against his natural instincts. But he ended the call and then sat down to work out how the contact could be carried out. It wouldn't be easy to do a standard brush contact because a BlackBerry was a fairly bulky device. Finally Danny came up with an idea.

He carefully wrote down Elena's instructions and added Deveraux's orders. Then he added a line of his own:

This one's from me. Always keep your passport with you for a quick getaway after the op.

He paused. He wanted to write something else, something more personal. Could he write 'Love, Danny'? He could feel the heat rising in his cheeks when he thought what Fergus or Deveraux would say about that. Wasting valuable operational time on mushy stuff, probably. 'Thinking of you'? 'I'm here for you'? No. Got to be professional. She knows I'm here. Leave it.

Briskly Danny folded the sheet of paper and put it into the film container.

He left his room and took the lift down to the eighth floor. The lobby area was deserted, but Danny checked the corridor before going along to the small room housing the vending machines. He slipped inside, pushed some coins into the drinks dispenser and bought himself a can of Coke. Then, quickly and efficiently, he pulled the small container from his pocket and ran one hand down the back right-hand edge of the machine until he found the hard strip of Velcro exactly where Elena had said it would be.

She had stuck the Velcro at waist height, so that if anyone came along and saw either of them at the machine, they wouldn't be scrabbling around on their knees or reaching up high. Danny quickly stuck the canister onto the Velcro pad and went back to the lifts.

He pressed the recall button, opened the Coke can and took a sip as he waited for the lift. The first part of the operation seemed to have gone, if not completely to plan, at least more or less OK, but Danny was still worrying about Elena as he rode down to the hotel reception. He swallowed the last of his drink and walked out through the revolving doors.

The street was even busier now, with New Yorkers and tourists rushing past, hunting for cabs or heading for the subway. Danny went over to the concrete rubbish bin just to the right of the main hotel doors. He dropped the Coke can into the bin and, with his free hand, unpeeled one of the red dots from the pack in his jacket pocket; he stuck it close to the rim of the concrete so that Elena would see it as she approached the doors to the hotel.

He was following the instructions Elena had given him in the canister. The system was simple: each time the DLB was made live by Danny, he would leave a red dot stuck on the bin. When Elena made the DLB live, she would leave a blue dot.

According to Deveraux, Danny's work for the evening was done.

But Danny didn't see it that way. He had other plans as he walked away from the hotel.

25

The Japanese restaurant was nothing like anything else Elena had ever experienced. She had never eaten Japanese food; she'd had Chinese, but that was usually from south-east London takeaways with their paper menus, Perspex-covered countertops, bottles of soy sauce in display cases and piles of freebie calendars decorated with lanterns and dragons.

The restaurant of the Mandarin Oriental Hotel was like another world. Elena had followed Black Star's instructions and taken a cab to Columbus Circle. She walked into the Time Warner Center and took the escalator up to the mezzanine.

The entrance to the Mandarin was close by, but she paused and looked back through the huge glass windows to Columbus Circle itself. It was a huge concrete roundabout where at least six roads met and spewed traffic away in every direction. At its centre was a twenty-metre-high granite column, topped with a marble statue of Christopher

115

Columbus. But Elena wasn't interested in Columbus; she was thinking of Danny, wondering if he was out there somewhere, looking out for her like he had promised.

Feeling very out of place, she walked into the Mandarin and took the elevator to the thirty-fifth floor of one of the two towers. She was welcomed at the door of the restaurant like a familiar and valued customer.

The restaurant was subtly lit and tastefully decorated, with panoramic views over Central Park and Manhattan Island. The tables were covered with white linen and immaculately laid, the cutlery nestling next to sparkling wine glasses. One wall of the room was entirely covered with rack upon rack of wine bottles.

Elena was shown to a secluded booth and informed that each course of her meal had been selected in advance.

As she waited for the first course, she glanced around the busy restaurant, feeling nervous and self-conscious. It was obviously the haunt of the wealthy and influential. Some diners were chatting loudly to each other, talking business deals; others were speaking on mobiles, texting, or even working on palm-top computers. Even though the working day was over in New York, it didn't mean that work ground to a halt.

Most tables had at least two diners, but Elena's eyes were searching for those eating singly. She picked out two men and one woman who were alone at their tables. The woman was elderly and heavily bejewelled.

There was no way she was Black Star.

One of the men was young, mid to late twenties,

using his chopsticks like they were welded to his hands, enjoying his meal down to the last few grains of rice.

The other man was older, dark-skinned and smartly suited. He was talking on a mobile phone but, like everyone else, appeared to be taking absolutely no notice whatsoever of Elena.

It was hopeless. Black Star was probably nowhere near the restaurant or even Columbus Circle, but even so, Elena constantly had the feeling that somehow he was watching her. Suddenly she became aware of English accents, loud English accents.

Across the room a group of mainly young men were seated around a large circular table. Their striped shirts and garish ties were as loud as their voices. Elena could hear them talking finance and deals and percentages and profit margins. It was obvious that they worked for one of the business organizations that had recently moved into the Columbus Circle complex.

One of the men, who appeared to have had too much to drink, began arguing with a waiter over a missing plate of prawns. 'Well, you make bloody sure they don't turn up on the bill when it arrives,' he said loudly. 'I'm in finance, you know. I check bills.'

Elena looked away. 'Prat,' she said to herself.

The waiter brought the first course; as he placed the dishes on the table, he saw Elena's look of confusion.

'Crab,' he said with a smile. 'Fennel and green almond mousseline, with blue crab consommé jelly.'

Elena tried to look as though she knew exactly

what the waiter was talking about as she nodded her thanks. He smiled again and moved silently away.

The food looked and smelled good, but Elena wasn't really hungry. With her body on UK time, it felt too late to be eating. She picked at the starter but soon pushed away the plate with most of the food still remaining, then got the BlackBerry out of her bag.

As she logged on, the waiter reappeared and glanced at her plate with a look of disappointment. 'You don't like crab?'

Elena smiled. 'It was lovely. I'm just not very hungry.'

The waiter shrugged. 'That's a pity; there are many more courses to follow. Perhaps the chef's lobster will tempt you. Or the suckling pig.'

He gathered up the plates and moved away. Elena looked at her BlackBerry as Black Star's first message appeared on the screen.

Hi Gola, so wot d'u think???

Elena looked around the restaurant again; everyone appeared to be having a great time.

Its very nice.

She could almost feel the rage in Black Star's reply.

Nice!!!!!!! Sure its nice!!! Cos those guys there r the haves. They got everything they want, they don't care about the likes of u & me. Nothing ever went wrong 4 those guys. Look at them,

118

smug, plenty of money, no problems, they got everything they want. But did one of them give u a second look, or even a smile????

The bile of Black Star's words hit Elena with a familiar jolt. This is what the last few months had been like, and the anger and hatred of their online conversations had gradually affected her mood. At first she had been a willing participant, but more recently—although she had never really admitted it to Dr Jacobson or even to herself—it had started to change the way she saw the world. And here it was happening all over again. She suddenly felt her spirits sink.

She looked around at her fellow diners, telling herself it was the tiredness that was making her feel so low, but then she found herself thinking that perhaps Black Star was right: they all looked ugly, wolfish, smug and self-satisfied in their own wealthy worlds. She tapped out her reply.

The waiter smiled.

Sure the waiter smiled—hes paid 2 smile. And even he wouldnt stop 2 help if he saw u injured in the street. Just wanted 2 remind you what a crap world it is, Gola. But we'll show em, Gola. U r the 1 with the POWER!!!

Elena moved the BlackBerry slightly as the waiter returned with a dish of lobster and noodles. He placed the dish on the table and turned quickly away. All at once it did seem to Elena that his smile was false. That he'd decided he'd done his best to interest her in the food on offer; if she wasn't

119

hungry, she shouldn't have turned up at the restaurant. Satisfied customers usually meant a good tip. She clearly wasn't a good prospect.

Ur right, this world is totally crap!!!

There was a delay of a few seconds, but then Black Star came back on a different tack.

Tell me, b4 u went into the Mandarin, did u c the elevators to ur right???

Elena thought back to her arrival.

Yes.

Good, remember them. I'll let u finish yor meal now. Will come back 2 u when u r at the hotel. I need 2 give u tomorrows shopping list!!!

*   *   *

Rain was falling steadily, making the road surfaces black and shiny in the lamplight, and the bright neon signs seemed to illuminate almost every building, when Danny got out of the taxi on the Central Park side of Columbus Circle.

The cab drew away and he pulled up the collar on his jacket and moved back closer to the edge of the park to escape the light. He had learned to make the best use of shadow. He looked over at the Time Warner Center. The central area was like a wall of glass. Danny's eyes moved upwards as he took in the two towers on either side.

The two massive buildings, all steel and glass,

mirrored each other in shape and design as they stretched upwards into the sky.

Danny had no intention of going into the restaurant, or even into the centre itself: that might compromise Elena. All he planned to do was wait until she emerged from the building and then follow her to the hotel, just to ensure she got back safely. There were plenty of yellow cabs cruising around this part of Manhattan. Danny would simply wait until Elena got into hers and then flag down another.

But in the meantime he needed to find a good vantage spot to watch for Elena as well as somewhere to shelter from the rain.

He kept his eyes on the entrance to the towers but moved slowly back towards the metre-high stone wall at the edge of the park, where the shadows were darker and the streetlights barely penetrated.

The rain was bouncing off the road and pavement and Danny didn't hear or see a thing when two arms reached out and grabbed him. One was clamped across his mouth and the other went round his middle, squeezing all the breath from his lungs, as he was dragged back over the wall and deep into the darkness.

*   *   *

Somehow, when the head waiter helped Elena on with her jacket and said, 'We hope to see you again very soon,' she didn't quite believe him.

She had hardly been a great advertisement for the chef's undoubted skills, and the long-suffering waiter had looked almost relieved when she asked

121

if he would mind calling her a cab.

The yellow taxi was waiting with its engine running and the rain bouncing off its roof. Elena hurried over and bent down towards the driver's half-open window.

'Hotel Pennsylvania, please. It's on Seventh and Thirty-third Street.'

'I know where hotel is,' said the driver gruffly in a heavy Eastern European accent. 'I drive cab, I know way around this town.'

Elena got into the back of the taxi and pulled the door shut without saying another word. It moved swiftly away, splashing through the kerbside puddles. She shifted into the middle of the back seat and pulled her jacket collar up around her neck, feeling very small and very alone. She would have given anything to have had Danny, even at his most annoying, sitting in the cab with her.

She glanced through the thick Perspex window between her and the driver and noticed the man's dark eyes staring at her from the rear-view mirror.

The loneliness tightened in her chest and a single fat tear rolled down her left cheek. Quickly she looked away, hoping that the driver had not seen.

'Listen . . . miss . . . I'm sorry, very sorry,' said the driver, looking in the mirror again. 'I'm not right to talk to you like that. I'm miserable man.'

Elena almost smiled as she wiped the back of her hand across her face. 'It's OK, it's not your fault. It's been a . . . a bad day.'

The driver nodded. 'You visit New York for first time?'

'Yes.'

'I drive you through Times Square. You must

122

see. Don't worry, no extra charge, it's on the way.'

Too tired to argue, Elena just slumped back on the shabby, ripped seat.

They were soon at Times Square, but then, caught up in traffic, moved across it at a snail's pace. It was ablaze with light from the hundreds of neon signs and giant screens advertising everything from Coke to the latest Broadway shows and movie releases. Elena had been impressed by London's Piccadilly Circus but that was nothing compared to this.

Thousands of people thronged the pavements and streets; cabs and cars jostled for position with two-seater pedal taxis and gleaming white stretch limos. Every tenth car seemed to be a stretch limo in this part of town.

Voices shouted and traffic cops' whistles screamed. A woman stepped off the kerb and almost got run down.

That's what it would be like, Elena thought. One minute alive, the next . . . not. A bang. Pain. And then . . . nothing. All these people, scurrying from one place to another. And what for? If death is the end for all of us, does it matter how it happens?

Elena's driver glanced into the mirror again to see if his customer was looking any brighter. She wasn't; she seemed to be a million miles away, deep in her own thoughts.

'Where you from?'

'England. London.'

'England!' said the driver, lifting both hands from the steering wheel for a moment and returning them with a thump that made the vehicle swerve across to the centre of the road. A horn blared and the cab driver made the single-finger gesture as another car passed his with only centimetres to spare. 'Maybe I should have gone to England instead of come here when I leave Russia.'

'Russia?'

'I live in Moscow. Until I come here with my wife and my two children.'

'Why did you leave?'

The driver laughed. 'For better life. Ha! It is joke. In Russia I have good job as engineer in factory. Not much money, but no one honest has money in Russia. Russian mafia, they have all the money. So we come here, start again. I'm lucky even to get this job. Live in stinking apartment, work every hour, never see my wife and kids and not enough money to pay even doctor's bills.'

The vehicle cleared Times Square and soon after it pulled up near the Pennsylvania. Elena paid the fare, then, as the driver gave back her change, she pushed it all back into his hands.

'They have saying here in America,' he told her. ' "Life is bitch, then you die." ' He looked at the tip Elena had given him and smiled. 'You have good holiday, miss.'

26

Danny was in the back of a hire car cruising past the Pennsylvania as Elena walked into the building. His ribs still ached and his face felt as though there was an imprint of a hand across his mouth.

Mick was not exactly the caring, sharing new-man type; he had not been gentle as he pulled Danny over the wall, and Fran's words had been

124

almost equally bruising once Danny had been bundled away from the surveillance area.

Fran was driving the vehicle and Mick was in the passenger seat; they carried on for a block before taking a left turn. 'You were told!' said Fran to Danny for the third time. 'You were told to stay away and you deliberately disobeyed orders. You could have compromised the operation.'

'Yeah, all right,' said Danny, pissed off with apologizing. 'But I didn't, did I? There was nothing to see.' He thought for a minute. 'I suppose I should have guessed that you two would be part of all this. Why didn't Deveraux tell us?'

The two agents exchanged a look. 'Because you didn't need to know until it was necessary,' said Mick. 'Who d'you think is here to take out the target when we get to him? You? Your little friend? It's our job. Taking care of business.'

Danny said nothing, but the thought struck him that maybe these two were not just here to take out Black Star. Maybe their business would not be concluded until they had also taken out Elena and him too. And what about his granddad? Maybe they had already . . . He pushed the thought from his mind; he didn't even want to go there.

Fran took another left; she was heading towards the rear of the Pennsylvania, and she was still fuming that Danny had risked compromising not only the surveillance, but the whole operation. She pulled the vehicle into the kerb, switched off the engine and turned in her seat to glare into Danny's eyes.

'Your granddad cost me a few busted teeth and Mick three cracked ribs last year. And he was also responsible for the deaths of two of our mates, with *your* assistance. So dropping you because you're fucking things up wouldn't cause me one moment's loss of sleep. You understand?'

Danny swallowed hard and nodded, but Fran hadn't finished.

'Good. So now you've had your horoscope read, you can get out!'

She started up the engine as Danny opened the door and got out. As soon as it was closed again, she shoved the vehicle into gear and roared away.

'Up yours,' said Danny as he headed for the hotel entrance.

*   *   *

Elena was close to exhaustion, but she had still remembered to check out the rubbish bin on the way into the hotel. The small red dot was easy to see, if you knew what you were looking for. It was about five centimetres below the rim of the bin, which was almost overflowing with discarded McDonald's cartons, drinks cans and paper cups.

When she reached the eighth floor, Elena went straight into the dispenser room, slipped some coins into the machine and pressed the button for bottled water. The machine thumped and the bottle thudded into the dispensing bay. Elena reached down and picked it up.

She stood still and listened. The only sounds came from the constant hum of the air conditioning and a slight buzz from the electric lighting.

Quickly she moved to the back of the machine and freed the small canister Danny had left for her. She opened it, pulled out the folded sheet of paper

126

and read the instructions.

Elena sighed. Even Danny's note at the end was just another order. So much to remember all the time. She gave herself a mental shake; too tired to think now. She needed some sleep, then her brain would start working properly again.

She jammed the container into her jacket pocket and ripped the paper into small pieces before shoving them into her mouth, chewing and quickly swallowing. It tasted foul, but she knew that with a few swigs of water it would be over in seconds.

When she reached her room, she let the door slam and then walked over to the window without turning on the lights.

She felt certain that Black Star was watching her, waiting for her to go online to receive her next set of orders.

But Black Star would have to wait—for a few minutes at least.

The New York skyline was ablaze with light; the varying shades of yellow, white and pale blue marking out separate buildings, roads, towers. Maybe a million lights were shining on the city.

But Elena wasn't looking at the lights. Her eyes were fixed on the steady flow of rainwater that streamed down the window just centimetres from her face.

Like tears, a flood of tears, washing everything away.

27

Dr Jacobson had spent a restless night; sleep was elusive and she had spent long hours trying to make a decision. She glanced over at the digital clock and saw that it was just after five a.m.

As far as she was concerned, Elena had coped incredibly well so far. But Black Star, whoever he might be, was extremely practised at grooming the teenagers he had chosen to be his Angels of Death. His subtle use of his victims' own anxieties, his powerful use of language, his caring and sympathetic tone wormed their way into his victims' psyche. He fed the wildest and most extreme feelings of self-loathing and hatred of the whole world into the teenagers' minds. And when he had them, he struck. He was a master of manipulation. And the pressure was difficult for even a well-adjusted teenager to bear.

But Elena, even with all her recent history, *had* endured it, usually without making the slightest fuss. Until the last couple of weeks. It wasn't surprising; Dr Jacobson would have been astounded if there hadn't been some reaction.

But she was worried now.

She came to the decision she had been wrestling with. She sat up, switched on the lamp and opened the single drawer in the bedside cabinet.

She lifted out the envelope that Elena had tucked into the battery compartment of her computer. It was still sealed, but Dr Jacobson had decided that she had to read the letter that Elena had written to her father.

It was a professional decision: she didn't feel right about reading what was obviously a very personal letter, but she had to know how Elena's mind was working. It was important—and not only for Elena's own safety.

Carefully she pulled open the sealed envelope as gently as she could, unfolded the single sheet of paper and then began to read.

Dear Dad,
I don't know when you'll read this, or if you'll ever read it, but I had to write down what I was thinking while I have the chance.

You've let me down, Dad—again and again and again. I really thought that this time, when we'd got to know each other more, you regretted the way you'd let me down in the past and that you were going to make sure we had a proper relationship in the future. Just a normal dad, that's all I wanted. Nothing extra special, or different from anyone else, just someone who I could talk to, who really cared about me, who wanted to be there for me when I needed him.

But no, you've disappeared again, just like before. I suppose I should have expected it, but I didn't, I really didn't. And that's what makes it worse this time. So much worse.

I still miss Mum, you know. Being the way I usually am, cheerful and all that, people think I've got over her dying. But I haven't. I think about her every day. I say

goodnight to her and tell her I love her every night before I go to sleep. I thought that you and me would be able to talk about Mum at some time, that maybe you'd be able to help me. But no, you've gone.

Danny's been a really good friend to me and we've talked sometimes, but it's not the same. I thought there was something special between Danny and me but it can't be the same as what's meant to be between a dad and his daughter. I suppose it was different when Danny and me both believed we were completely alone—it was stronger between us then. But he's got Fergus now, so I suppose he's got something like I hoped to have with you.

Also, Danny's really wrapped up in all this stuff we've got to do. It's changed him. He forgot my birthday—everyone forgot my birthday. I know you always forget my birthday, but it didn't stop me doing this really stupid thing. I kept looking out of the window, sort of expecting you to turn up with a card and a present for me. I knew you wouldn't—you don't even know where I am—but I still kept looking, and hoping. All day, until I went to bed. And then I cried. I do that a lot lately and I hate myself for it.

Anyway, Dad, the real reason for this letter is to tell you that I do love you and that I forgive you. You are what you are, Dad. I know you'll never change now. I wanted to say these things because I'm

**going away tomorrow and I don't think I'll
ever see you again.**

**So take care, Dad, and remember,
I LOVE YOU.**

Your daughter,

**Elena
xxx**

Dr Jacobson was a professional, and one of the
rules of her profession was never to become
emotionally involved. But as she refolded the letter
and slipped it back into the envelope, her eyes were
misting with tears.

She got out of bed and reached for her mobile
phone. It was very early, but Dudley, if he was
sleeping, was about to get a rude awakening. He
had to know about this. It was imperative.

28

Paddington Green Police Station, on the Edgware
Road, is one of the main holding bases for possible
terrorists or other high-risk suspects when they are
taken into custody. It is like a fortress.

Fergus was being held there. At Heathrow he
had been bundled into a windowless white transit
van and then taken directly to Paddington Green.
There, the wagon was driven through an archway
and into a lift, which slowly descended into the
bowels of the building.

No charges were made, no explanations were given, but Fergus didn't expect any. He knew the routine. All the way from Heathrow he had been silently cursing himself for not anticipating this move. Deveraux had stitched him up good and proper and there was nothing he could do about it. But *that* didn't bother him; not being in New York to protect Danny and Elena did.

Fergus had read every one of Deveraux's sit reps for Dudley, and almost every one had reiterated that she wanted them dead. Danny and Elena were aware of the danger, but Fergus had reckoned on being there to get them out when the moment came.

But he wasn't there. Instead he was stuck in a London cell with no chance of escape.

Years earlier, Fergus had been incarcerated in a Colombian prison and had organized and led a mass breakout. That had been difficult; breaking out of Paddington Green was impossible.

His possessions had been taken away and he was ordered to change into garish yellow overalls and to put on a pair of thin slip-on shoes with elasticated sides. He did so without complaint; there was no point in complaining.

Then he was locked in a small purpose-built SSU. It wasn't a home from home. Despite government legislation that all cells should have some form of natural light, this place had none. It couldn't have—it was deep underground. The electric lights were recessed into the ceiling with thick wire running through the glass.

There was a single bed, fitted to the wall, and a stainless steel toilet with a push button flush system, also set into the wall. There was nothing

132

for any prisoner to rip away for use as a weapon. The cell was the ultimate holding pen. Even if a prisoner scratched paint from the wall, the guards would be alerted by the cell's hi-tech alarm system.

With no natural light as an aid, Fergus was finding it difficult to keep track of time. The guards wore no watches when they came in with bread and water. And when food did arrive, Fergus knew it wasn't at normal meal times—that could also have been a guide to the time. It was all part of the process of keeping a prisoner disorientated.

Fergus had eaten everything given to him apart from one small corner from a slice of bread. Bread usually goes a little hard around the edges after an hour and completely hard within twenty-four. It was Fergus's rough guide to the passing hours.

He was desperately worried, not for himself, but for Danny and Elena. He was tired now, but he had to stay alert and try to figure out some new tactic.

As he turned over on the uncomfortable bed, he heard the cell door being unlocked. Fergus got up, expecting to see at least two police officers entering.

It was Dudley.

They looked at each other for a few moments before Fergus spoke. 'Come to gloat? Or do you want to tell me what you've got in store for me? Don't bother, I know.'

Dudley looked around the cell as if he was expecting to see somewhere to sit down. The bed was the only option so he remained standing. 'This is unfortunate, Mr Watts, I agree, but it was considered necessary.'

'Yeah, I bet it was. Your idea, was it, or *Miss* Deveraux's?'

133

Dudley shrugged his shoulders. 'That isn't particularly relevant now. There have been developments, Mr Watts.'

Fergus felt a surge of panic. 'Danny—something's happened. Is he hurt? Or Elena . . . what is it?'

Dudley reached into the left pocket of his overcoat. 'They're safe for the moment,' he said as he drew out the now crumpled envelope containing Elena's letter. 'But I want you to read this.'

Fergus grabbed the envelope and pulled out the letter. He read it through; Dudley waited in silence until Fergus looked up at him. 'Where did you get this?'

'It was hidden in Elena's computer. Dr Jacobson is of the opinion that Elena may be considering—'

'Going through with what Black Star's telling her to do,' said Fergus quickly. He gripped the letter tightly, crumpling the paper even more. 'I should have seen this. I should have known what was happening to her.'

'Hindsight is a wonderful thing, Mr Watts, but that doesn't help us now. You know her better than we do. *Could* she go through with it? Dr Jacobson feels that the letter—and Elena's recent mood—suggests—'

'It doesn't matter whether she *could*—we've got to make sure that she *doesn't*.' Fergus stared hard at Dudley. 'I can stop her.'

Dudley raised his eyebrows. 'You can? How?'

'Elena will never trust Deveraux, never. If she's really thinking of going through with this, then Deveraux won't even get near her. Elena trusts me, just me and Danny, and you can't expect Danny to do this. I can *do* it, so get me out there.'

134

Dudley considered for a moment. 'Dr Jacobson concurs, which is why I'm here. I have found her opinions remarkably accurate in the past and I see no reason to doubt them now.'

He paused. 'Miss Deveraux disagrees, naturally.'

'Who gives a shit what she thinks! Look, all you care about is the mission, and not having American body parts flying around if Elena detonates the explosive. I'll stop that, and you'll still get Black Star.' Fergus glanced at Elena's letter again and then held it up to Dudley. 'And this—it was a waste of time. Joey's dead, isn't he?'

Dudley shrugged again with a gesture that said it was something that could not have been avoided. 'That last night . . . He was taken. A little later and it might have been different.'

Fergus nodded. He knew the realities of the business they were in and the rules by which they operated. 'And Deveraux did it?'

'You know I can't tell you that, Mr Watts.'

'You don't need to.'

'And you don't need me to tell you, Mr Watts, that ours is not one of the caring professions. But it's a necessary one, vital for the security of our nation and the world. And had you been in the same position as the person who carried out the act we're discussing, then you know perfectly well that you, as a professional, would have done exactly the same thing.'

Dudley was right. Joey had been just another innocent victim of the game they all played. It had happened before and it would happen again.

Fergus nodded. 'Then it's even more important that you get me out there now. Don't you realize what will happen if Elena does detonate the IED?

135

To you?'

Dudley's eyebrows rose again. 'Me?'

'You! The man who authorized a British covert operation in the USA that the Americans didn't know a thing about, which went completely wrong and resulted in the deaths of maybe hundreds of US citizens! Oh, I know it's Deveraux's mission, and it's deniable. I've been there, remember? But the Americans won't be letting you walk away from this, Dudley. They're no fools, they won't swallow the deniable line for something this big. This will come all the way down from the President, and he'll want more than Deveraux. You're her boss. They'll have your bollocks on a plate.'

Dudley swallowed hard as the image was conjured up in his mind.

'Before agreeing to let you go, I want your absolute assurance that you will not attempt any acts of revenge, or tell Elena that her father is dead. That information could initiate the very thing we're attempting to avoid. Do I have that assurance?'

Fergus nodded once. 'Like you said, I'm a professional.'

'What do you want?'

'The operation *is* deniable, right?'

'Under the circumstances, it has to be.'

'Then I'll need a Tornado to get me there quickly and some RAF cover. I need a small dip bag and I'll have to go back to Oxford to pick up some kit. You can organize a fast car to take me there and then on to Marham.'

'Kit, Mr Watts?' said Dudley. 'Can't we supply you with what you want?'

'Not with what I need. I have to go to the hotel.'

'If you're talking about a weapon—'

'I don't need a weapon; I'm going to save her, not kill her. Now let's stop talking and get on with it.'

29

Elena had hardly slept. The thought that Black Star might be watching made dropping off to sleep difficult. At around two in the morning she finally realized that Black Star himself must have to sleep at some time, and after that she dozed fitfully.

She was up early. She switched the TV to C-SPAN and watched the news for a while, then hauled herself wearily out of bed and went into the bathroom, washing and dressing quickly. The thought that Black Star could be watching her even there was not pleasant. She left the TV on when she left the room.

Hanging the DO NOT DISTURB sign on the handle of her door, Elena wondered briefly how far Black Star's surveillance reached. There was no one in the corridor, but could he be watching her there as well? All the training she and Danny had had from Fergus meant that she knew she could not afford to relax, to be herself, for a moment. She had a part to play and had to play it one hundred per cent—everywhere. A single slip could blow the operation. So much relied on her to get it right.

As Elena walked along the airless corridor towards the lift, the enormity of the task hit her. Her heart began to race and she felt she could hardly breathe. The trip down to the lobby seemed to take ages. She felt sick and tired and her head was throbbing, and at that moment she would have given anything to be back home at Foxcroft with Dave and Jane.

The fresh air coming into the lobby from the street revived her a little. She was sitting in the coffee shop at the front of the hotel with a latte and an untouched blueberry muffin twelve minutes before the contact time Danny had stipulated in the instructions she had found at the DLB.

Sipping the latte, Elena had a moment of panic: she suddenly realized she should have left a message of her own at the DLB that morning, giving Danny details of Black Star's orders. But she had forgotten. Black Star had given her the first of her shopping locations, the time she was meant to be there and details of what she was to buy. That information should have been passed on.

How could she have forgotten? If this had been a test, she would have failed. But this was no test— it was for real. Elena realized that there was no time now for her to find somewhere private to write a note, go back up to the eighth floor, leave it at the DLB and get back down to stick a marker outside for Danny before he turned up at the coffee shop.

Her mind was racing. She had at least remembered Danny's instruction to pick up a giveaway magazine on her way into the coffee shop. She opened *Welcome to New York, the Big Apple* at a random page and attempted to look as though she was casually flicking through as she enjoyed her breakfast. Then she closed the magazine, took a pencil from her jacket pocket and began to write on the front cover, hoping it looked like she was

138

just making a note of something of interest within its glossy pages.

*   *   *

Danny reached behind the drinks dispenser on the eighth floor and found there was nothing attached to the Velcro. Elena had obviously taken his message last night, but for some reason had not left one of her own with Black Star's latest orders.

He had begun to worry when he went out early, bought a pretzel and a coffee from a stall on the street corner as a cover for checking the rubbish bin, and saw that there was no new 'DLB live' marker.

But he was still checking the DLB, assuming that Elena had gone off SOPs and had left a message without leaving a marker. But there was nothing. He was starting to flap as he checked his watch. It was 08:20—ten minutes until his scheduled contact—and he had no idea if she would be there.

At 08:00, exactly on schedule, he had taken a call from Deveraux, who prevented him from asking about Fergus by giving him a string of orders about where to deliver the BlackBerry once it was in his hands. The ear-bashing he'd had from her about his activities at Columbus Circle the previous evening still smarting, Danny listened in silence.

'And there's something else,' she went on before Danny could mention his grandfather. 'You are to take over surveillance of Elena today; I need the other two for something else. I want to know where Elena is, what she's doing and who she meets. Surveillance, Danny, that's all. Report to me.'

She hung up without mentioning Fergus. The

139

morning had not begun well.

Danny decided to risk going off SOPs and walked past Elena's room to see if there were clues to whether or not she had followed any of his instructions from last night. He began to feel a little better as he approached the door. The DO NOT DISTURB sign was plainly visible.

As he passed by, he stopped and went down on one knee, pretending to retie his trainer laces. The sound of droning voices just filtered through the door. It had to be C-SPAN; politicians always sounded boring.

So Elena *had* acted on his instructions. But why hadn't she left a message of her own? Maybe she had; maybe the container had slipped away from the Velcro and fallen on the floor behind the vending machine.

Danny got up and went back to the DLB. He pushed himself up against the wall and attempted to look behind the machine. All he could see was electrical wiring and the casing for the dispenser's cooling system.

'Come on, Elena, where is it?' he whispered. He dropped to his knees and reached as far as he could along the gap between the wall and the back of the machine, but still found nothing.

He crawled around to the side and slid his right hand underneath the machine. Still nothing. Gradually he moved round to the front, each time sliding his hand as far as he could beneath the dispenser in the increasingly vain hope of finding the plastic film canister.

And then the door opened and a middle-aged man walked in. He stared at Danny, looking puzzled. 'Lost something?'

Danny smiled weakly; his hand was pushed in so hard it was almost jammed under the machine. 'I dropped my money—a quarter.'

'A whole quarter?' said the man, feigning horror. 'And you can't find it?'

Danny shook his head, feeling as stupid as he looked, and pulled his hand out from under the machine. 'I don't have any more cash, not until I go to a cash point.'

'Well, it's lucky I was passing and saw you scrambling about on the floor,' said the man, reaching into a pocket. 'We can't have you going thirsty, can we? You look as though you need a drink after all that effort.' He held out a coin.

'No. No, I couldn't,' said Danny, scrambling to his feet. 'It's really nice of you, but—'

'Look, I insist,' said the man firmly. 'We Americans pride ourselves on being hospitable to our overseas visitors.' He grinned. 'Specially our poor relations from across the pond.'

He pressed the coin into Danny's hand. 'You Brits just kill me,' he said with a smile, then turned and headed back into the corridor. Danny had no alternative but to slip the money into the machine while he waited for the man to reach the elevators. He checked his watch again: 08:26—only four minutes until he was meant to make the contact.

Quickly he ran to the fire escape and hurtled down the stairs, taking three or four at a time, desperately hoping that Elena would be waiting for him in the coffee shop. If she wasn't, none of Deveraux's orders of last night could be carried out, and Danny had a pretty good idea who would be getting the blame for the cock-up.

But as he ran down towards the lobby, it wasn't

141

Deveraux he was worried about, or even himself. It was Elena; he had promised he would be there for her at all times.

In the coffee shop Elena was kicking herself for being so dumb, and mentally running through her options. But so much relied on everyone following SOPs, sticking to the training, following the practised moves. And she'd blown it right at the beginning. She started to feel sick again. Perhaps, she thought, if Danny turned up, everything would be sorted. She checked her watch; it was 08:31. Danny was late.

Elena's breakfast things had been cleared away. She couldn't sit around for much longer; Black Star had given her precise instructions on the timing of her first shopping venture. She glanced towards the entrance of the crowded coffee shop and almost smiled: Danny was there, with a bottle of water in one hand. He was breathing deeply and Elena saw a bead of sweat trickle down one side of his face.

As soon as she was certain that Danny had seen her, she got up and walked quickly out of the restaurant. She couldn't go back now. She had to keep going. And hope.

Danny looked over to the place where Elena had been sitting and instantly spotted the magazine on the tabletop. It was folded down the centre, just as he had instructed.

He began to move towards the table; slowly, not rushing, remembering his grandfather's training: be third party aware and always have a reason for doing whatever you do.

Casually he sauntered towards the table. It was free; he would take it. But then, when he was just a couple of metres away, a woman came bustling by.

She reached the table and slid her tray onto it, then turned and smiled at Danny. 'Mine, I think.'

Danny was completely unfazed. 'Sure—I just left my magazine behind.' He reached out and grasped the folded magazine firmly, feeling the BlackBerry Elena had tucked inside. As he picked up magazine and BlackBerry, he grinned at the woman. 'Have a nice day.'

He moved away, heading for his RV. He left the hotel, carefully slipping the BlackBerry out of the magazine and into his jacket pocket. And as he continued along the street, he unfolded the magazine and saw Elena's handwriting on the front. He smiled with relief; he knew where she was going.

'Next time, Elena,' he breathed, 'stick to SOPs!'

*　　　*　　　*

Deveraux's plan for uncovering Black Star's identity and location was three-pronged, with each member of her team playing a role in the high-speed operation.

Elena was central to the operation. She was the focus for Black Star and, through her, Deveraux was certain she could reach him.

The first part of the plan was to get hold of the BlackBerry that Black Star had given Elena. All the information stored in its memory needed to be downloaded and analysed. And even if that information gave no clues to the location of Black Star, the technical experts on hand at the British Consulate still had a job to do. Deveraux wanted to be able to see and read every future online conversation between the target and his latest recruit. The experts could fix that.

Secondly there was the surveillance system that Black Star had almost certainly rigged in Elena's room. There could be a miniature camera or two and microphones. He'd probably used the television. It was the obvious place, and in the past Deveraux had rigged many such devices herself. Black Star was known to be a technical expert and would be using state-of-the-art kit. But Deveraux had a plan to turn this to her advantage.

Thirdly there was Elena herself. She had to be followed and watched without Black Star realizing that she wasn't operating alone as he thought. That had been the responsibility of Fran and Mick, but now they would be employed on a job requiring even more experience and expertise. They would be attempting to locate and penetrate Black Star's suspected hotel surveillance system. If they were successful, they were likely to find Black Star a lot sooner than anyone would by following Elena.

Deveraux had watched Danny during the training period and knew that, when he focused, he was able to follow a target without being pinged. Now the skills that he had practised and honed under his grandfather's instructions were about to be put into practice, although this time it was no test run; there could be no mistakes.

The job was his, but first he had to deliver the BlackBerry for downloading and then return it to Elena. He walked round to a prearranged meeting place at the rear of the hotel, where Fran and Mick were waiting in their hire car.

Danny opened the nearside rear door, got into the car and handed the BlackBerry to Fran, who was in the driver's seat. Without a word, she quickly slipped a mini jack plug into the device. The USB connection on the other end of a short lead was connected to a small laptop computer.

The download took just seconds, and while Fran watched its progress on the computer, Danny read the few words Elena had written on the magazine.

'Black Star's told her to go to a drugstore called Duane Reade,' he said as he read. 'She's given me the address and directions.' He looked at Fran.

Fran looked back stonily. 'Well?' she said.

'I'll have to get a cab.'

'Then get one.'

Fran pulled the jack plug from the BlackBerry and handed it over to Danny. 'Get this back to her. And don't be seen doing it.'

Danny had no idea how he was going to manage that little miracle, but he leaped from the car without another word.

The two operatives watched him hail a passing yellow cab. Then Fran passed Mick the laptop and started up the engine. 'We'll get that over to the Consulate—then we can start playing hunt the C-SPAN channel.'

'Yeah.' Mick grimaced. 'Or the needle in the haystack.'

30

This was Black Star's day.

The day Pointer had dreamed of for over five years. Once it was over, he would continue with his acts of revenge for as long as he could, but this was the special one. The one that counted the most.

145

He had almost lost the precious opportunity. Two months earlier, the Angel he had long been grooming for this special day suddenly went cold on him. He had been very surprised. It wasn't the first time an Angel had been abandoned during the grooming process, but it was a long time since that had happened. In the early days he had lost a few by pushing too hard, going too fast for the fragile personalities who fell prey to his insidious words, or just by misjudging the character of his victim. More recently he had become much more adept at grooming. Now he was confident that he knew exactly what his Angels were thinking. Once he got them to a certain point, they were completely in his power and his revenge would follow in the most bloody and horrific way he could devise. That was the sweetest feeling, the balm for the pain in his soul. So, after the successes in London and the other cities, it was most disappointing to lose one. It was a crushing blow.

All those months of slow and careful preparation had been lost. Wasted. And there was nothing Pointer could do about it. He knew there was no point using his limited time trying to find out what had happened. Pushing a reluctant victim was useless. His success, his whole method of operation, was based on exactly the opposite. He pulled. Slowly, gently, tugging his victims into exactly the position he wanted. But on that occasion he had failed.

And then Elena had come along, at precisely the right moment. When he was helping her to reach information via the Deep Web, Pointer had only considered her as a potential future Angel.

But once she had slipped back into his net, he

had worked quickly, more quickly than he would have wanted. The grooming and preparation process would normally have taken much longer. But Pointer was lucky. He could tell from the beginning that she was close to the edge, and it was easy to work out what emotional buttons to push to bring her into his power. She was perfect. His special Angel for this special date.

He knew that speeding up the grooming could be a risk, but it was one that he had to take. There was no time to test her resolve, and there was still a chance that, if she stopped and thought about what was going to happen, Elena too would pull out at the last minute. Pointer considered the risk to be small—he was certain that he had her completely under his control—but one which he was going to cover. He would not give her time to think. To reconsider. She was tired; he would keep her that way. And keep her on the move, frantically busy with the preparations for tonight's main event.

Because tonight Black Star's special Angel was to die.

*　　　*　　　*

Duane Reade was doing good business, even though it was still early. It was like a cross between a British Boots and a mini supermarket, with aisles packed closely together and shelves stacked to overflowing. According to Black Star, this was just the first of a number of stores Elena would be visiting throughout the morning.

She collected a plastic basket and took out her preliminary shopping list. She had to be quick: Black Star had warned her that she would be operating to a tight schedule and that he would be coming online at various times during the morning with further instructions.

And there was the problem. She didn't *have* the BlackBerry to receive those instructions; Danny had it. At least, Elena *hoped* he had it.

As she went in search of the first item on the list, a sports bag, all she could do was pray that Danny had picked up the BlackBerry and magazine and then read her scribbled message. If not, she was in trouble.

She located the sports bags and chose one that was folded flat and wrapped in its packaging. Next on the list was a pair of rubber washing-up gloves. She found them and slipped them into the basket.

There was just one further item to find at this first stop. She went to the aisle where the drugs were stacked and picked out two big 'family' tubs of aspirin and then made for the checkout.

The assistant raised his eyebrows when he saw the two big tubs. 'That's a lot of aspirin, miss.'

'They're for my dad,' said Elena. 'He has a heart condition.'

The assistant smiled sympathetically and ran the first of the tubs over his bar code checker next to the till.

Black Star had anticipated the question and provided Elena with the answer. As always, he had thought of everything.

*   *   *

The cab was still a block from Duane Reade when Danny heard the beep from the BlackBerry.

'Oh, no,' he breathed as he glanced at the screen

148

and saw Black Star's message.

Hi, Gola, hows it going? U got everything so far?

'Shit!' Danny thought quickly: he couldn't just leave the message unanswered. Black Star would suspect that something was wrong. His thumbs went to the keypad.

Just about.

Two words were as much as Danny felt he could risk, but Black Star came back immediately.

Great. Ur going somewhere more interesting next. Bergdorf Goodman on 5th Avenue. Theyre waiting 4 u at the Dolce & Gabbana stand. Everything bought and paid 4 but they might have 2 make a few small adjustments. Will do them 2day and deliver 2 hotel later.

The cab pulled in to the kerbside and Danny thrust some dollars into the driver's hand. Without waiting for change, he jumped out of the taxi and walked as calmly as he could into Duane Reade. *Third party aware*, he said to himself as his eyes scanned the shopping area. *Stay third party aware.*

Elena had bought and paid for her goods but didn't know what to do next. If she left the store, she had to go somewhere; she couldn't just hang around. But where would she go? Back to the hotel? Another store? Which store? She was hoping desperately that Danny was on his way with the BlackBerry now. All Elena could think of doing was to play for time. She stopped by a display case of photographic equipment and just stared at it, seeing nothing.

She hadn't moved when Danny spotted her. His first instinct was to go straight up to her and hand over the BlackBerry. But he knew he couldn't do that. He had to stick to SOPs.

His eyes scanned the shop floor as if searching for a particular item. People were browsing, reading labels, selecting, most of them on the move, making their choices.

But then Danny's eyes rested on one particular man. He was at the end of an aisle on the far side of the store from Elena. He was standing completely still. Watching Elena. There was no doubt about it. He was watching Elena, waiting to see what she did next.

Danny was certain it was Black Star. It *had* to be. He was staring at Elena because she wasn't responding to his last online message. But she couldn't; Danny had the BlackBerry.

Danny came to a stop in front of rows and rows of shampoo and hair conditioner, keeping one eye on the man, who turned round and started to make his way towards the exit. Danny attempted to take in as many details as he could as the man moved away. Face, hair, height, build, clothes.

The man walked through the main doors and Danny decided he had to make his own move. There was no other choice. He turned and headed towards Elena. As he got closer, his hands wrapped around the BlackBerry in his jacket pocket.

Elena saw Danny reflected in the glass of the display cabinet. She began to turn, not knowing what to do. But before there was a chance to say or do a thing, Danny walked straight into her.

'Sorry, sorry,' he said, as though it was a complete accident. With one hand he grabbed Elena's shoulder, making it look like he was trying to stop them both from falling; the other went into a pocket of Elena's jacket. She knew then that Danny was returning the BlackBerry.

'There's two messages—I've replied to the first one,' whispered Danny, their faces just centimetres apart. 'See you there.'

Elena nodded and Danny turned and walked away.

Outside, he looked up and down the crowded street to see if the man was still around. There was no sign of him. Danny began looking for a cab as he pulled out his secure mobile phone and punched in Deveraux's number.

The call was answered immediately. Danny could hear that Deveraux was in a moving car. 'Yes,' she said.

'I got the BlackBerry back to Elena.'

'Good.'

'Yeah, but there's more. I think I've just seen Black Star.'

'You *think*? What do you mean?'

'This guy in the store. He was staring at Elena.'

'That doesn't mean a thing. Men stare at women. Haven't you noticed?'

'But . . . but it was more than that.'

'What? What did he do?

'Well . . . he stared, and then . . .'

'Yes?'

'Well, he . . . he left the store.'

Danny could hear the doubt and scepticism in Deveraux's voice. 'Give me a description.'

'Middle aged. Black hair, streaked with grey. Medium height. Wearing a dark blue, bomber-style jacket and light trousers. Couldn't see his shoes. I only got a quick look, but his face was . . . darkish. Maybe tanned . . . I dunno, South American? Or Mexican . . . yeah, Mexican.'

31

'Diplomatic bag' is a catch-all expression which all governments use to their advantage when moving secret items into another country.

A diplomatic bag may well be exactly that: a bag containing top secret documents. But it is just as likely to be a sealed box or even a freight container.

What is important is that diplomatic bags, of whatever shape or size, are untouchable. They are classed as the sovereign soil of the country they belong to, in exactly the same way as an embassy or consulate.

Marcie Deveraux had used the security of the diplomatic bag system to bring into the USA the items she believed would be necessary for the operation. These included weapons and various items of kit. They were taken straight to the British Consulate on arrival at JFK airport.

Since then, a consulate courier had delivered those items to Deveraux at the Four Seasons, and she in turn had passed some of them to Fran and Mick. Foreign Office couriers are trained to just do their job and ask no questions. They make deliveries; they even make collections of information left by double agents in DLBs. But when they are doing so, they never have any information on the operation itself.

Fran and Mick were now using radio scanners as they attempted to locate the listening device they suspected was in Elena's hotel room.

The scanners were each about the size of a paperback book. Fran and Mick were walking around the block in which the hotel sat, working a little distance from each other. Both had their devices in a pocket and were using Bluetooth, with an earpiece in one ear as they listened to all the radio, mobile phone and even secure traffic in and around the hotel.

As they had both said earlier, it was a little like hunt the thimble, but if the hunch about the camera and microphone in the room was correct, and the signal was being picked up and beamed out towards wherever Black Star lurked, then they could well detect it. That was the theory anyway.

In the meantime they had to listen to, identify and dismiss dozens of random calls and communications. Everything from cab drivers to cops, to the occasional snippet of a supposedly secure conversation between US secret agents working undercover on a drugs bust.

They were attempting to pick up the sound of the C-SPAN political TV station, which, they hoped, was being transmitted out of Elena's room by a hidden microphone. If Elena had followed orders, she had left her TV set switched on and tuned to that channel. It was highly unlikely that any other tourists would be watching it. Hardly anyone did, even Americans, as it featured only political issues, mainly coverage of endless government committee meetings.

But importantly for Fran and Mick, it wouldn't be confused with anything else they might find on their scanners.

Mick smiled as he picked up more of the Net surveillance chat between two US drug enforcement officers as they closed in on a suspected dealer somewhere in the immediate vicinity.

But there wasn't time to take any more than a passing professional interest in the drugs bust. Fran and Mick were on the trail of a mass murderer.

*   *   *

It wasn't the first time Fergus Watts had made a supersonic flight across the Atlantic by Tornado jet. But he had been a little younger and a lot fitter on the previous occasions, and the rear seat in the cockpit was cramped and uncomfortable. Particularly as Fergus's injured leg was giving him hell. But as always, he didn't complain.

The hours had passed swiftly. Fergus had left Paddington Green Police Station in an unmarked police car and was driven at high speed, firstly to the hotel in Oxford and then on to RAF Marham in Norfolk.

Four motorcycle outriders escorted the police car, leapfrogging ahead of each other as they ensured that junctions and any potential hazards were clear so that the vehicle could speed through.

The stop at Oxford was brief. Fergus's luggage had been recovered from Heathrow Airport, but all he wanted now was a few essentials, which he shoved into his rucksack, and the small bag of dull white powder, which could now be carried safely

154

into the USA under the total protection of the dip bag Dudley had provided. Within minutes he was back in the car and the high-speed journey resumed.

At Marham, the vehicle was driven straight up to the Tornado, and Fergus quickly clambered into a flying suit and helmet. The pilot was already in the cockpit, going through his pre-flight checks. He nodded a welcome as Fergus climbed in behind him, and within minutes the jet was moving towards the runway.

The fuel pods beneath each wing were completely full, enabling the Tornado to make the two-and-a-half-hour flight across the Atlantic without the delay of a mid-air refuel.

It thundered down the runway and rose into the sky as Fergus listened to the conversation between pilot and control tower. The Tornado climbed steadily, and just after it had crossed the west coast, Fergus heard the boom as the jet went supersonic and broke the sound barrier.

They were flying to Francis S. Gabreski Airport at Westhampton Beach, Long Island, New York, the home of the 106th Rescue Wing, New York Air National Guard. The airport was just a ninety-minute drive from the city.

Fergus glanced down through a clear sky to the deep blue sea far below. He was on his way. At last. And as a supposed member of a Royal Air Force aircrew, he would have his passport stamped with a visa and be heading for the city without having to go through customs. Even more important was the dip bag; Fergus was relieved he would not be required to explain the contents of that to anyone.

Deveraux was waiting. She had driven out from the city to meet Fergus personally, having argued unsuccessfully with Dudley against him being there at all.

She sat in the comfortable back seat of the Consulate's limo, deep in thought. Dudley had told her exactly why he had agreed to Fergus flying out to join the mission: there was a strong possibility that Elena might actually have succumbed to Black Star's grooming—and he put the success of the operation above everything else.

Deveraux had asked whether or not there had been a rethink as regards the ultimate fate of Fergus, Danny and Elena and Dudley had stressed that there was no change to the plan.

'In fact, Marcie,' he had told her, 'given the apparently fragile state of Elena's mind, I'm even more in agreement with your recommendation. They would almost certainly pose a grave security risk in the future.'

Deveraux was at least glad to hear that. She could have gone on about the apparent lack of faith in her ability to run her mission, but she chose to remain silent.

She would turn this to her own advantage. She hadn't wanted Watts here, but perhaps he might indeed be able to stop Elena going flaky on them if things got tough. And at least Danny would stop moaning about his grandfather now.

But Deveraux wouldn't stand for Watts getting all holier than thou with her over the killing of Joey Omolodon.

She knew that Fergus was now aware of the

truth—Dudley had told her so. It didn't matter, as long as he didn't try to preach at her or, even worse, threaten to let Elena in on the secret. That would most certainly mess with Elena's mind and therefore jeopardize the entire operation. Then Black Star would be lost.

Deveraux sat weighing up the possibilities as she gazed around the airbase. It was relatively quiet; many members of the 106th were on active duty out in Iraq, and it looked as though a skeleton staff was keeping the airport operational.

Deveraux checked her watch, having almost convinced herself that Watts would not be stupid enough to attempt any crazy acts of revenge. But when things got personal, even the hardest, coolest operator had been known to do the unexpected. She would have to watch him. And, if he got in the way of the mission, kill him before it was over.

The Tornado was due in within the next few minutes and Deveraux ran through the events of the past few hours, including Danny's supposed sighting of Black Star. That boy had too vivid an imagination, but at least he was sticking to orders now.

Deveraux glanced skywards, ready now to remind Fergus that even though he had found a way of getting involved, this was still her mission and he was there in an advisory capacity only.

Her Xda rang. 'Yes, Fran.'

'We've picked up the TV channel. We have a footprint of the signal—he's not far away.'

'Good, well done.' The scream of a Tornado coming in to land made it impossible to speak for a few seconds. But as the aircraft touched down and continued along the runway, the noise began to

157

diminish. 'Do what you have to do and then call me with a sit rep.'

Deveraux ended the call and smiled. If Fran and Mick struck gold, Fergus might well be sitting in the back of the Tornado by the time it was ready for its return journey to the UK.

32

Elena was not really surprised when she arrived at the Dolce & Gabbana stand in Bergdorf Goodman and was presented with a beautiful, black, fitted designer trouser suit and a crisp white shirt to try on.

Nothing was surprising any more. She was moving in a fog of exhaustion and anxiety. The friendly assistant told Elena that she knew she was in a hurry and ushered her towards the changing room. Elena forced a wan smile in return.

'I'll look after that sports bag if you like,' the assistant said as she went through the white louvred door.

It took a lot for Elena to say, 'No, it's all right, I'll keep it with me.' It was easier now just to do as she was instructed, or ordered, but she guessed that Black Star would not want the bag out of her sight for even a moment. Knowing that he was probably watching her even now, she accepted that he was the one who mattered most.

The assistant simply smiled tactfully and moved away. In the privacy of the changing cubicle, Elena slumped for a moment, leaning her aching head against the cool of the mirror, and allowed her eyes to shut. But only for a moment or two. There was a job to be done. Slipping into an outfit worth more than all the clothes she had ever bought for herself was strange for Elena, but no stranger than everything else that was happening.

*   *   *

Danny walked past the Dolce & Gabbana stand and continued on past small concessions with Italian-sounding names he had only vaguely heard of. He was sticking carefully to SOPs: always have a reason for whatever you do. He was ready with a story about looking for a birthday present for his girlfriend if anyone asked.

He had followed Elena into the beautiful art deco store, every fibre concentrating on staying third party aware. He knew that he might not be the only person watching Elena. Even though Deveraux had poured scorn on the idea that the man he had seen earlier was Black Star, Danny thought differently. He was looking out for him again, convinced that he would see him, and ready to prove Deveraux wrong.

If he did spot the man again, Danny had a further idea. He figured the best way of keeping tabs on Elena would be to follow the follower. That way, he would be in control of the surveillance. And while he was at it, he planned to snatch a photograph of his suspect with the camera on his mobile phone.

But first the man had to turn up. And so far, he hadn't.

*   *   *

Inside Dolce & Gabbana Elena emerged from the changing cubicle. The sales assistant was good at her job, ignoring the vacant look on her client's face.

'Oh, it looks as though it was made for you. Beautiful. And the knee-length jacket suits you perfectly.'

It did look good, but Elena had taken no more than a glance at herself in the mirror in the changing room.

She had the weirdest feeling of being somewhere else, as though she was watching the scene play out on a screen far away. She watched this other Elena standing perfectly still as the sales assistant asked her to hold open the jacket while she made a few checks. 'Maybe just half an inch shorter in the legs and a tiny bit off the waist. You're so slim.'

Elena forced her mind back to the present. 'I've lost weight lately.'

'Well, don't you go losing any more; you're just perfect as you are. The jacket is generously cut; it's meant to look like that. If you'll just slip back into your own clothes, we'll make the adjustments and have everything round to your hotel by early this afternoon. You'll look *wonderful*. Is it for a special event?'

Elena nodded. 'Yes.'

She went back into the changing cubicle and was stepping into her jeans when the BlackBerry gave its now familiar beep.

OK, Gola, time 2 move again. U need 2 go 2 another drugstore. Ready 4 instructions????

Elena started. So Black Star had to be here, in the store somewhere. Even here, he was watching her. As she emerged from the cubicle, she looked around, but there was no one she recognized.

$$* \qquad * \qquad *$$

A few minutes later Danny watched her head towards the store's exit. There had been no sign of the mystery man so he had no alternative but to follow Elena.

Outside, she hailed a cab. Danny shouted down the next cab he saw, got in and ordered the driver to 'Follow that cab!'

'Which one, buddy?' said the driver, turning back to look at him. 'Or you just making like you're in a movie?'

Danny stared out through the windscreen. There were three yellow cabs up ahead of them on the street. Danny pointed at the one he thought Elena was in. 'That one!'

The driver shrugged, shoved the vehicle into gear and pulled away from the kerbside.

Danny had been unlucky. Only a few seconds later Herman Ramirez walked out of the store with his cell phone to his ear.

33

Fran and Mick's scanners had locked on to the signal coming from the television set in Elena's hotel room. The task now was to find where it was being beamed to.

It couldn't be far, within a block or so at the most. They had to discover where the beamed signal was strongest.

They walked away from the hotel in separate directions, both apparently listening to music on an iPod. In fact they were listening to a congressman from Texas as he attempted to explain the intricacies of a proposed budget deficit. It was all waffle to them both, but all that mattered was keeping his boring voice droning on in their earpieces.

They were walking the footprints of the signal. When it grew weaker, they would turn round, search for the place where it picked up, then walk in another direction until the signal became weaker again.

Gradually they were reducing the search area and getting closer to their target. Closing in on Black Star.

The congressman was booming in their earpieces as they met each other. They were on the ground floor of a multi-storey car park. And whenever they walked away from the car park, the signal became weaker. This was it; he had to be here.

They moved into the ground floor of the concrete structure and, one after another, using the cover of parked vehicles, they checked weapons— the HK P11s that Marcie Deveraux had brought into the country in the diplomatic bag.

The P11 was rarely used; it was a strange, futuristic-looking weapon, which was made in two parts and was battery operated. The chunky five-round barrel unit slotted into the pistol grip section, where the batteries were located.

All five chambers were visible at the front of the barrel unit, but until the moment of firing, each chamber remained tightly sealed. This was because the weapon was designed to be used underwater, where it had an effective range of ten to fifteen metres. It had been invented primarily for use by divers taking out other divers.

Electricity continues to work underwater, and the pistol used an electric current to fire the bullets from the barrels in the same way as a detonator is used to kick off explosives.

The barrel held not only the five rounds but also the charge that fired the round. This was released when the trigger was pulled, sending it to small connectors at the back of the barrel. The electric current detonated the explosive charge behind the round and it was fired. The round itself was dart-shaped, to glide through the water more efficiently.

Out of the water, the P11's range increased to thirty metres, more than enough for Fran and Mick's requirements. And the bonus was that the P11 was virtually silent and the 7.62x36-calibre rounds would have a devastating effect on the target.

Slowly and cautiously they began checking vehicles. They were fortunate: it was mid morning by now and the car park was virtually full, so there was little traffic moving about. Or people.

They were looking for a vehicle that was big enough to conceal someone watching and listening in on Elena's room.

The ground level was clear and so was the first. But on the second floor, as they worked their way along the rows of vehicles, Fran stopped suddenly and drew Mick's attention to a blue van parked thirty metres ahead of them.

Gradually they edged closer, each pulling on two pairs of surgical rubber gloves. They had bought the cheap gloves, which split very easily, from a 'dollar store'. The double layer would ensure that no prints were accidentally left on a vehicle.

Their eyes searched for the tell-tale signs that someone might be hiding inside the vehicle: condensation on the windows at the front, slight movement of the vehicle as someone shifted inside. There was nothing, but they both knew that it didn't mean the van was unoccupied.

As they moved closer and were able to see into the front, they spotted that it was blocked off from the rear of the van; someone could easily be concealed in there.

They reached the vehicle and eased their way along the bodywork to the rear doors. Mick pressed one ear up against the closest door while Fran stood on stag, watching for anyone approaching.

Mick could hear nothing, but he still wasn't sure.

And then the sound of men's laughter startled them both. They moved away just as the doors to the stairwell were flung back and two construction workers, still wearing their yellow hard hats, came bursting through.

The joke must have been good because they kept laughing all the way to the van. One of the workers had keys in his hands. He opened the driver's door and climbed in, and as Fran and Mick moved on to the next level, they heard the van's engine start up and the vehicle pull away.

'Thought we had him there,' said Mick as they climbed the stairs.

'We'll get him soon,' said Fran.

But they found nothing until they reached the top floor. And then, stepping into the open, they spotted something that was surely what they were looking for.

Parked in one corner was a large Winnebago with two small satellite dishes on the roof. One of these was pointing directly towards the hotel and the other was aimed in the opposite direction. All the curtains at the Winnebago's windows were drawn, even the ones dividing the driver's seat from the rear of the vehicle.

Fran and Mick inched closer to the vehicle until, weapons up, they reached the side door. They stopped and listened. There was no sound. Nothing. After a couple of minutes Fran reached into her jacket, took out a Leatherman and pulled the knife from its sheath.

Mick, still with his weapon up, was covering Fran as she gently worked the blade into the gap between the door and the bodywork. Within seconds she had forced the lock.

She flung back the door and stood aside as Mick burst into the wagon and went right. Fran was immediately behind him. She went left and they stood their ground inside the wagon, weapons up, ready to drop anything that moved.

But there was no one inside the vehicle. Instead, Fran and Mick immediately saw a suitcase-sized machine on the Winnebago's dining table. Two sets of wires came from the back and went out through the roof to the two satellite dishes.

'The bastard's using a rebroadcaster,' said Fran as she pulled her mobile phone from her pocket.

From his study in The Hamptons, Pointer watched
as Fran punched in Deveraux's number. Hidden in
the Winnebago was another tiny camera. It had
been fitted by Herman Ramirez for just such an
eventuality.

Pointer watched Mick inspect the rebroadcaster
and then begin to check out the Winnebago's
cupboards and drawers. The bomb master frowned
as he pondered exactly who the two uninvited
visitors were. He knew they would find nothing in
the vehicle that would help them.

But who were they? Police? FBI? CIA? Did they
know about Elena? The pistols they held looked
highly unusual. And how had they found the
vehicle?

He allowed himself a slight smile. It didn't
matter now. None of it mattered. He had always
known this would happen eventually. Some form of
law enforcement agency was closing in on him. So
what? Tonight was the night he had waited so long
for. This would be the last one, the one that really
mattered. By the time they found him it would be
too late. His beloved son would be finally, and
spectacularly, avenged.

*   *   *

Marcie Deveraux and Fergus Watts were treating
each other with what might best be termed as
'professional respect'.

Fergus had decided during the flight in the
Tornado that he would say nothing to Deveraux
about the fit-up at Heathrow. For one, it had been

166

a job well done, and Fergus had a grudging respect for that.

For two, he didn't want to antagonize Deveraux any further and possibly alert her to his own plans. And for three, Fergus just wanted to get on with the job in hand.

So he made no mention of Deveraux's killing of Joey Omolodon, but simply reiterated Dr Jacobson's concerns about Elena's mental state. When they discussed the letter Elena had left for her father, he didn't refer to the fact that Joey would never read that letter. It was almost as if he were still around, but missing.

Deveraux was more than a little relieved: they didn't have time for recriminations. In return, she brought Fergus fully up to speed on developments since their arrival in New York. She even spoke of Fran and Mick's role in the hunt for Black Star just as if Fergus had known about their involvement all along.

Fergus nodded but made no comment. Without spelling it out, Deveraux had revealed to him who was on hand to carry out the actual killing of Black Star. And Fergus didn't need telling that they were also around for when Deveraux decided that he, Danny and Elena were no longer needed.

They were both being polite and professional as the limousine arrived back in the city and headed towards the Four Seasons.

And then Deveraux's Xda rang.

'Yes, Fran?'

'We've found a vehicle. There's a rebroadcaster. The signal's being encrypted and sent out by microwave.'

Deveraux sighed with irritation and considered

167

for a moment. 'I suppose we shouldn't be surprised—he was never going to make it easy for us.'

It was a blow, but as Deveraux had said, not completely unexpected. It meant that the signal was being received in the Winnebago and then sent on to another receiver. Black Star might be at that location, but it was equally possible that the signal was going on to another rebroadcaster. And then another. And another. For all they knew, Black Star could be way up north, in Canada.

The rebroadcaster boosted the strength of the encoded signal, and this could be sent onwards over long distances. The only thing in the hunters' favour was that the microwave operated within a narrow band and the dish had to point in the direction in which the signal was being sent.

Deveraux knew that. 'You'd better start playing dot-to-dot.'

'Yeah,' answered Fran, 'I thought you'd say that. Could be a long job.'

'Give me the details of the wagon and we'll check it out. We're closing in on the bastard.'

Deveraux noted down the details as Fran gave them to her and then ended the call. She quickly relayed the facts to Fergus.

'Doesn't make me feel a whole lot better about Elena's safety,' he said. 'Where is she now?'

'She's shopping.'

'And what's she buying?'

'Black Star's got her running all over the city. Danny's doing his best to keep track of her, but he's on his own while Fran and Mick chase Black Star, so—'

Deveraux's Xda rang again. It was Danny.

'Yes, Danny?' She put the Xda on speaker mode.

'I've lost her. I followed her in a cab to another drugstore. She was buying aspirins, candles . . . other stuff. It's definitely mix thirty-nine. But then she took the subway, and by the time I'd got a ticket she was gone. There was no way I could stay with her.'

Deveraux took the news well; she hadn't expected Danny to be able to stay with Elena indefinitely. 'At least we know what she's doing. Go back to your hotel and leave a marker and a message for Elena. Tell her we need any information she can give us through the DLB.'

'But I don't want to just sit around waiting,' said Danny urgently. 'There must be something else I can do.'

'Yes, there is, Danny,' said Deveraux curtly. 'You can follow orders. Now get back to the hotel and wait.'

Fergus butted in. 'Danny?'

'You're here!'

'Of course I'm here,' said Fergus, glancing towards Deveraux. 'Look, don't worry, we'll get Elena through this.'

Deveraux cut the call; there wasn't time for family reunions.

'I need to be at the Pennsylvania with Danny,' said Fergus. 'If Elena starts mixing when she gets back, it means the attack is on today. I have to be at the hotel.'

'And what can you do there?'

Fergus had no intention of telling Deveraux about the powder sitting in his dip bag. 'If you and your team get to Black Star while Elena's mixing, I can get her out of there and make the mix safe.'

Deveraux knew that Fergus was right. It was the best use of his skills; it was what he was here for. But for now she wanted Fergus where she could see him. They were nowhere near to catching Black Star yet, and for the moment, even with the concern about Elena's state of mind, while they had her under surveillance she was safe enough. If they tried to get close enough to talk to her, they risked blowing the whole operation.

'No,' she said without looking at Fergus. 'You stay with me until I say otherwise.'

Fergus sat back and said nothing. He had read Deveraux's sit reps: he knew exactly what she wanted for himself and Danny and Elena, once Black Star was dead. But he didn't know what Dudley's response had been to Deveraux's recommendation, although he could make an educated guess: 'Recommendation for elimination approved.'

He almost smiled at the irony of it all: while Black Star lived, so did they.

34

Elena finally returned to the hotel after her shopping expedition, carrying two bulging carrier bags and the new sports bag, which was full to bursting. She had moved beyond any normal concept of tiredness now and felt strangely but distantly alert. Detached from everything except what she had to do. It was the feeling she'd had in Dolce & Gabbana, but now it was there all the time.

Black Star had warned her that there would be further items for collection at the hotel reception. She trudged up to the desk and gave her name and room number. 'I think there's something for me to collect.'

'Gee, that's a lot of souvenirs to take back home,' said the receptionist, looking at her shopping bags as he handed over a carrier bearing the Dolce & Gabbana logo, along with another brown padded envelope with Elena's name typed on the front. 'You're gonna have to pay big time excess baggage on that.'

Elena couldn't even be bothered to reply. She smiled weakly, slipped the envelope into one of her shopping bags and continued over to the lifts. She was expecting Black Star to come straight online as soon as she entered her room. And he did.

U done good, Gola, real good, & I no ur tired. But dont worry, a few more hours & this will all b over. I need u 2 do exactly wot I say from now on and be REAL careful as u work. OK?????

Watching her from his desk many miles away, Pointer was tempted to tell Elena to switch off the television set, which was still tuned in to the C-SPAN channel, but he had more to think about than his Angel's viewing habits. It was possible that Elena suspected he was somehow watching her, but he wasn't going to confirm that. Not yet. Not until it was necessary.

As he considered this point, Elena seemed to realize for herself that the TV was still on, blaring out unwanted news. She walked over to it, giving

Pointer a close-up view of her exhausted face, switched it off and then went back to the BlackBerry.

Yes, ok.

Good, now 1st i need u 2 get everything out of the bags and lay it on the bed. Make sure the do not disturb sign is on yor door.

Already is!!

Pointer had instructed Elena to buy everything that was necessary to make mix thirty-nine. She looked at the strange assortment of ingredients: aspirin tablets . . . tubs of Vaseline . . . bottles of rubbing alcohol . . . packs of candles . . . even a jar of sulphuric acid, which she had obtained from a hardware store. She had also bought a set of kitchen scales and electric rice cookers.

When everything was laid out on the bed, with the rice cookers and scales on the floor, Pointer was ready for Elena to begin preparing the instrument of her own death, and the death of many others.

He had to work quickly; the device would take around three hours to complete but could not be rushed. One wrong move could end in disaster, and the years of planning and preparation would be wiped out in an instant.

Ok, lets go. First, this stuff is gonna smell bad and its gonna get hot, so i want u 2 put the aircon on cold—full blast. Close the curtains, then get a spare blanket from the cupboard and shove it in the gaps around the door so the smell dont get outta the room. We dont wanna give no warning of wot we're doing.

In her room, Elena suddenly went cold. So this was it.

Her heart pounding, she thought quickly. She knew she had to concentrate and follow her instructions methodically, almost robotically, obeying Black Star's orders to the letter. Not giving away for one moment that she knew anything about PE.

Ok, Gola, put on the rubber gloves. We gotta crush all those aspirin. Take around 50 to start with and fold them in a sheet of newspaper and I'll tell u wot 2 do next.

Elena reached for a tub of aspirin and a sheet of newspaper.

*   *   *

Fergus and Deveraux were in the suite at the Four Seasons, and they had just received news of a vital breakthrough.

No attempt to trace the identity of the owner or hirer of the Winnebago could be made through US Security Services because the entire operation was deniable.

But MI6 officers back in London had been working overtime to find the missing details. And they had struck gold.

They had traced the vehicle back through the number plate and discovered that it was one of five purchased recently and registered to an address on the Upper East Side of Manhattan.

The vehicles were registered in the name of a film company at that address. But further checks had revealed that the film company had never made a single film, or been in any way involved in one. All the company had ever done was buy the Winnebagos.

The company secretary was listed as a man called Herman Ramirez, who apparently lived at the same address. Further undercover searches had revealed his driver's licence. Fergus and Deveraux were now staring at a photograph of Ramirez, which had been lifted from the licence, on Deveraux's laptop computer screen.

'Perhaps I should have had a little more faith in Danny,' said Deveraux as she looked at the face on the screen.

'What do you mean?' said Fergus.

'He said he thought he saw a Mexican following Elena. He was right—we have Black Star.'

Fergus was never easily convinced, and he was too concerned about Elena's safety to make any comment about Danny's surveillance skills. He nodded towards the computer screen. 'What else do we know about this guy?'

'Nothing. Nothing at all. Before this, he doesn't appear to have existed—not in the US, anyway.'

As they stared at the computer screen, Deveraux's Xda rang.

It was Fran. 'We've found another Winnebago. Rebroadcaster, same as before. This could take a long time.'

'Forget it,' said Deveraux quickly. 'I have an address for you. The Penthouse, Wiltshire

Buildings, East Ninety-sixth Street. The name is Ramirez. Herman Ramirez. You know what you have to do.'

* * *

Elena reacted like a rabbit caught in the headlights of a car when she heard the knock at her door. She froze, her eyes wide with fear.

She had been totally absorbed in following Black Star's instructions, working for over an hour as quickly as she could, following every order exactly. She had been careful to make a few unimportant mistakes, to hesitate occasionally. Black Star had been quick to correct her, repeating instructions until he was sure she had got it.

The explosive was gradually being created, with ingredients measured out in precise quantities and added carefully to the deadly brew.

The air conditioning was going at full blast but the room was still hot and the atmosphere was thick with pungent fumes as the mixtures in the rice cookers were slowly heated and reduced. Elena's eyes were streaming, there were beads of perspiration on her forehead and she was fighting to stop herself from gagging as she breathed in the toxic fumes.

But she worked on, following every instruction to the letter, horribly fascinated now at what she was cooking up.

And then came the knock at the door.

Elena stared, wide-eyed, at her BlackBerry, somehow expecting Black Star to tell her what to do. But nothing appeared on the screen: she had to sort this for herself.

'Hello?' she called.

'It's the maid. I need to do your room.'

Elena tried not to breathe too deeply as she thought of what to say. 'I don't want my room cleaned, thanks. Not today.'

There was a pause as the maid outside the room attempted to weigh up exactly what was happening on the other side of the locked door. 'Are you OK in there? There's a kinda strange smell. Like . . . like cooking.'

Elena stared at the rice cookers with their evil, slowly heating concoctions and said the first thing that came into her head. 'It's a burger. I brought it back with me, but it was horrible, I couldn't eat it. Actually, I don't feel too well.'

'No? You want me to call a doctor?'

'No, really, I'll be fine. I just need to sleep.'

There was another pause. 'And you're sure about the room? I'll have to report it to my supervisor if I don't clean the room.'

'I'm certain. Thank you. And thank you for your . . . your concern.'

'No problem. Hope you're better tomorrow.'

Elena stood up, went to the door and put one ear against it. She could just hear the cleaning trolley moving away down the carpeted corridor.

As she turned back, she heard the BlackBerry ping. She picked it up and looked at the screen.

Well done. Lets get on, shall we??? Time is tight!!!

At that moment Elena knew for certain what she had suspected all along: Black Star was watching her. And listening. She punched some words into

176

the BlackBerry.

Ur watching me arent u???

There was a pause and then Black Star came back.

Sure I am. Im looking out 4 u! U ok with that???

Elena smiled. She knew what to say.

Yes. Im glad. Makes me feel better.

35

Herman Ramirez had never questioned or challenged his master during their long campaign of revenge.

If ever the tiniest seeds of doubt about what they were doing crept into his mind, he would think of Chuck. He would, by now, have been twenty-two, through college and starting out on his career.

Chuck had been a good-looking boy. There would have been girlfriends, parties, vacations. Money would never have been a problem, so the growing-up years of discovery would have been full and exciting.

And then later Chuck would probably have married and there would most likely have been children. And Herman would have been part of it. He had looked forward to it all with huge anticipation when Chuck was alive. He had thought about it often then and he thought about it often now.

Herman had never been part of anything until he had come to be accepted and adopted as one of the Pointer family. He had no recollection of any family of his own, having been abandoned as a baby on the streets of Mexico City.

He had been taken into an orphanage but had run away as a nine-year-old and had lived on the streets, scraping an existence in whatever ways he could.

As a child, a teenager and an adult, he had never encountered very much in the way of kindness. It didn't get any better after he made the decision to cross the border into the USA illegally, where his solitary existence continued to have no real purpose. Until the day he knocked on the door of the Pointers' house in The Hamptons to ask if the family needed a general handyman.

Then his life had changed completely. For the better and for ever. It was good. It was better than good: it was more than he had ever imagined possible.

Until September 11 2001.

Since then there had been only one objective to life: revenge.

There had never been a moment of regret about the bombing campaign, nor the slightest trace of sympathy for the victims. Until today.

Herman had followed Elena all over Manhattan, watching her every move and reporting back to his master at each stage.

She had looked forlorn and lost as she hurried closer and closer to her own death. And something about Elena's vulnerability and isolation had touched a raw nerve deep inside Herman.

After he had watched Elena return to the Pennsylvania, he found himself a diner, where he sat and had a meal. He was off duty for a little while, knowing that Elena was in the hands of his master.

And as he sat and ate, he began to wonder about the strange and unfamiliar thoughts that were troubling him. He made his way back to the penthouse apartment on East 96th Street—where he would change, ready to go and observe Elena's final act that evening—still trying to work out why he felt unsettled.

It was only when he stepped out of the elevator and removed the keys of the penthouse from his jacket pocket that he finally realized what it was that had led to these feelings: Elena reminded him of himself as a small child, alone on the streets.

That was all it was. He felt better now that he had worked out exactly what had been troubling him. There was no room in his mind for anything but what had to be done. He was focused again and could make his regular report to his master and continue with his preparations.

He paused at the door to the penthouse, took out his cell phone and punched in a number.

'Yes?'

'I'm back at the penthouse now, sir, and will be ready in time to make sure she keeps the appointment.'

He slipped the key into the lock, turned it and pushed open the door as he listened to the man he had always admired more than anyone he had ever met. The man he would willingly, even happily, die for.

'Elena will be ready too,' said Charles Pointer II. 'I'm watching her now. Everything is on schedule.'

Herman walked into the penthouse and pushed the door closed. 'I'll call when I am ready to leave. Are there any further orders, sir?'

'No. Just do exactly as we have discussed. Just be there and inform me when she has gone into the building. I anticipate the television news will be broadcasting our success soon after. That is all.'

Pointer hung up even before Herman had pressed the END CALL button on his cell.

Herman slipped the phone back into his pocket and decided that he would take a shower to wash away the grime of a day spent walking around the city.

Then, from the rooms on either side of the wide corridor, there were two flashes of movement.

Before Herman could even register what was happening, a man and a woman were standing there, both with strange-looking, wide-barrelled pistols pointed at his head.

'Don't move!' shouted the man, who was closest to Herman. 'Don't move one fucking muscle!'

He slowly edged closer to Herman, making sure that the woman, who was a little further back down the corridor, had a clear view of the target so that, if necessary, she could get a head shot in.

Herman watched the P11 pistol come closer and closer to his head, unafraid but intrigued by its strange appearance. He could clearly see the five chambers at the end of the barrel.

He realized that the end of the pistol somehow reminded him of a tiny version of the Gatling guns he had seen in old western movies, with a US cavalryman operating a mechanical winder spewing

180

out round after round at the enemy as a long belt of bullets was fed through the weapon.

'Who's this "Sir" you were talking to?' shouted the woman, edging forward so that she could take the phone from Herman's pocket.

The man moved the weapon even closer to Herman, until it was jammed hard against his face.

If Herman could have smiled, he would have. He was content. At peace. His only regret was that he would not, after all, see the spectacular events of that night. He wouldn't be there now, but it didn't matter—he was only ever meant to be on hand in case of an emergency. But there would be no emergency. Elena would make her way there, just as his master had planned. She was completely in his control; Herman had seen that for himself throughout the day.

And so Herman was ready, and his attacker had actually made it so much easier for him . . .

*   *   *

Before Mick could pull back, both Herman's hands went up to his, grabbed them and forced his trigger finger backwards.

One round was instantly fired with a dull thud, smashing completely through Herman's head and burying itself deep in the wall behind him.

The only other sound was of Herman's body being hurled against the wall and slumping down onto the blood-spattered carpet.

'Shit! Shit! Shit!' yelled Mick as he watched the Mexican's body writhe out its final death throes.

'The phone!' shouted Fran. 'Get the phone! He was taking orders from someone else. He's not

36

A brand new Xda, identical to the one Deveraux already had, was on the pale wooden tabletop in her suite at the Four Seasons. The hinged top was open so that the screen was visible.

A technician attached to the British Consulate had just left the room after powering up the Xda and logging on to the website Black Star was using. Technicians—like couriers—were always in the dark when it came to helping out on an op. They just followed orders.

It was vital that Deveraux's own Xda was free at all times for calls to and from her team, so the technician had provided an identical machine which would be permanently linked to Elena and Black Star's online conversations.

The young and enthusiastic technician had begun to give Deveraux a detailed explanation of exactly how he had managed to hack into the system, using and processing the information downloaded from Elena's BlackBerry. But if he was expecting praise, he didn't get it. As soon as the machine was operational, Deveraux dismissed him curtly. She wasn't interested in *how* it worked, only that it *did* work.

Fergus's skills with mobile communication devices were limited to making and receiving calls, so he had been provided with a bog standard but secure mobile phone like Danny's.

Seconds after the slightly disgruntled technician

left the room, the Xda was showing absolute confirmation of what Fran had reported in a phone call to Deveraux just a couple of minutes earlier: Herman was not Black Star because Black Star was still communicating online with Elena.

Ok, Gola, we're nearly there. U made the mix real good, now u gotta go get some ice from the machine in the corridor. I no there is one, I checked it out. B careful when u leave the room. And get plenty of ice.

Deveraux turned to Fergus. 'Ice?'

Fergus's face had gone deathly pale. 'She's mixing. It's happening tonight—I should *be* there!'

'We wait!' snapped Deveraux. 'We cannot afford to alert Black Star by bursting in on Elena!'

The seconds turned to minutes as they waited for the next message to appear. While Deveraux stared at the Xda screen, Fergus got up and paced anxiously about, trying to ease the throbbing pain in his leg. A flight across the Atlantic in a confined space had done nothing to help the injury.

'She's back,' called Deveraux, and Fergus moved across the room as quickly as he could to stare at the screen.

Got the ice. Wot do I do with it???

Go into the bathroom. Put the plug into the sink and pour in the ice. Then u need 2 pour the contents of the 2 bowls onto the ice. The fumes r gonna be a nightmare so u need 2 get out quickly and close the bathroom door. Wait 10 minutes, then go back and u should see yellow crystals.

'That's it!' shouted Fergus. 'Those crystals are pure explosive! She's got another couple of hours' mixing and maybe three or four while the mix holds its detonating velocity. You've got to find Black Star soon or she'll be walking around the city with all that crap strapped to her body!'

*   *   *

As the afternoon sun hit the darkened study windows, Charles Pointer frowned: he'd just heard a soft ping from his computer. It had happened on each of the last three occasions he had sent or received a message, and each time the pings had been slightly louder.

During his career Charles Pointer had been a universally acknowledged master of computer technology and software development. Where he led, others followed. He had designed and built the system he was using now, and it was unlike any other in the world.

His computer was his weapon of war, with unique defence software, his own form of armour plating in the event of an attack.

He knew without doubt now that his system was under attack and that his armour plating had been pierced in some way. They were closing in on him. First there had been the break-in at the Winnebago, and now this. But there was still no need to panic; Pointer's computer was designed to turn defence into counter-attack.

Another message came through from Elena, and

with it came the accompanying, slightly louder ping.

Done it. It stinks, can hardly breathe in here.

Don't worry, it will clear soon. Just keep the aircon working and let the ice do its work. U'll need 2 do this maybe 4 times 2 get the amount of yellow stuff we need. So go get more ice and b careful!!

37

Danny had had it with being patient. And he'd had it with following orders. He'd done exactly as Deveraux had instructed by leaving a 'DLB live' marker and a message in the DLB for Elena, but had got nothing in return.

He had waited for more than an hour before revisiting the DLB, but there was no message from Elena. Her room was just down the corridor, and he desperately wanted to know what was going on in there, but he realized that if he went and knocked on the door he might very well endanger Elena's life.

Danny knew that Black Star almost certainly had some sort of surveillance system operating in Elena's room. And although Deveraux had kept him strictly on a need-to-know basis as far as information was concerned, he had figured out for himself that Fran and Mick had somehow been trying to locate that system.

That was why he'd been given the surveillance

job, and he'd done it to the best of his ability. But now he was doing nothing again. And Danny hated doing nothing.

He was back in his room, staring out of the window, down at the Manhattan traffic streaming past the hotel, trying to decide whether or not he should call Deveraux and his grandfather again.

His mobile phone was in his hand and he was itching to punch in Deveraux's number. But somehow he resisted the urge. He turned away from the window and picked up the key card for his room. All he could do was take another look at the DLB.

He decided to take the emergency stairs again, figuring that if he took the lift from his floor, it would look odd to anyone else when he got out on the eighth floor. The only reason for doing that would be if he knew someone on the eighth floor, and as far as any third party was concerned, he knew no one. SOPs were now almost second nature to Danny—when he decided he was going to stick to them.

The stairwell was cold and draughty, and Danny counted the floors as he moved down, his trainers making virtually no noise on the concrete steps.

He reached the eighth floor and paused, then looked through the wire-meshed, heat-resistant glass of the small rectangular window. He could see no one walking along the carpeted corridor. Danny pushed open the door and stepped through.

Then he froze.

Elena was standing at the door to her room. Clasped to her chest with one arm was what looked like two large paper cups filled with ice. She had just used her key card to unlock the door and was pushing it open when she glanced to her right and saw Danny.

She stared at him, then smiled briefly and went into her room.

Danny was still trying to work out if there was something more he could have done when his mobile phone rang. He pulled the phone from his pocket as he moved back into the stairwell and then answered the call. 'Yeah?'

Fergus's voice was little more than a whisper. 'Danny, it's me.'

'Granddad! I saw her; she's OK.'

*   *   *

Fergus was in the bathroom of Deveraux's suite, attempting to keep his voice as low as possible. 'Good news,' he said, relieved to hear that Elena was surviving the poisonous fumes which he knew would be filling her room. 'Now, listen up. She's mixing, so we've only got a few hours before the attack and Deveraux hasn't got to Black Star yet. I've got the powder with me; we have to try to get it to Elena. I know she's being watched all the time, but she might be able to add it to the mix. It's worth a go. So where do we RV?'

He nodded as he listened to Danny's instructions. 'Good, I'll be there soon. Wait out.'

He closed down his mobile and flushed the toilet and then went back into the sitting room, where Deveraux was watching the messages between Black Star and Elena.

*   *   *

Pointer's hands were moving swiftly on the computer keyboard as he calmly sought to pinpoint the source of the attack on his machine. The technicians at the British Consulate may have been good, but compared to Pointer they were like kids at primary school . . .

*   *   *

Deveraux and Fergus had no idea that the hunted was becoming the hunter. Fergus was more concerned about Elena. 'We've got to pull her out of there now.'

'No,' said Deveraux. 'Not yet. Fran and Mick are tracing the Ramirez call through ECHELON. We'll find Black Star and get him soon. If we pull Elena out now, he'll know we're onto him. She has to continue.'

The ECHELON computer, which collected all the electronic information zipping around in space from phone calls, texts and e-mails and sent it back to earth to be stored in huge computer mainframes, was already pinpointing Herman's calls and tracing precisely where those calls had been received.

But Fergus was old school. Technology had moved on hugely since he had been active in the field, but first and foremost he still trusted his own skills, experience and instinct. 'That stuff she's making is totally unstable—it could detonate at any minute. We have to get her out.'

'No!' said Deveraux sharply. '*I* command this mission, Watts, remember that. Elena is safe enough. The other IEDs remained stable until they were detonated. We're sure that the Williams

188

incident in Pittsburgh was user error; nothing to do with the device. Black Star knows exactly what he's doing.'

*   *   *

Black Star *did* know exactly what he was doing. In every way. As Fergus and Deveraux fell silent and stared at the Xda on the table, they were totally unaware of the almost inaudible click that came from the machine.

In the bottom right-hand corner of the Xda was the lens of the inbuilt video camera. It could be used for making short video movies or for video conference calls. But Pointer had almost effortlessly hacked into the PDA and had found his own use for the camera.

As the Xda made the single, almost silent click, a video picture of Fergus and Deveraux staring at the machine appeared in the top right-hand corner of Pointer's computer screen. And not only could he see them, he could also hear every word they said, as soon as they spoke. It wasn't as good as the set-up in Elena's room—the range of the mic would only allow him to hear conversation close to the Xda—but it was adequate for his purposes.

'Good afternoon,' he said softly. 'Welcome to my world. And what, I wonder, have you got to say for yourselves?'

As if on cue, Fergus turned to look at Deveraux, and as he spoke, his words were perfectly clear.

'Once she's got enough crystals, he'll tell her how to use candles and Vaseline to make it into PE.'

Pointer smiled. 'Bravo. You obviously know what

you're talking about, whoever you are.' His hands went back to the keyboard as he prepared to type out another message for Elena. 'But I think that from now on I will allow you to know only some of what I have to say to Elena. Just to keep you where I want you.'

He began to type.

Ur doin well, Gola. U ok???

Pointer watched Fergus and Deveraux exchange a look as they attempted to figure out Black Star's next move.

OK.

Elena waited and Fergus and Deveraux waited, but only Elena could hear the deep, calm voice that came from the speaker in the television set in her room.

'Hello, Elena. Don't be alarmed. It's me, Black Star. I'm here for you.'

She stared at the blank television screen. Pointer watched her carefully on his monitor. He knew the words would be so clear that it would seem almost as though Black Star was there in the room with her. He made his voice warm and comforting, although he knew it would not be what Elena had expected.

Elena didn't seem frightened, just startled. She smiled. 'Can you hear me too?'

'Sure I can. Hear you and see you. Are you OK with that?'

Elena nodded, clearly puzzled. 'You sound older than I thought you would.'

190

'*Yeah, I know. Are you OK with that too?*'

'Yes. But why are you speaking to me now, after all this time?'

As Pointer sat in his study staring into Elena's eyes, he felt a sudden flicker of doubt.

His enemies were closing in. Somehow they'd got close enough to target the communication between Elena's BlackBerry and the secure site. He didn't have time to find out how. Clearly their technical resources were almost as good as his.

He had to focus on Elena. He was so certain she was his. And yet he wanted to hear Elena *say* she would go through with it. She had to tell him.

'*Two reasons,*' he said softly. '*Firstly, we're very close now. I need to know that you really believe in what we've been talking about all these weeks. I need to know that you really want to do what we've been planning.*'

He saw Elena hesitate, and then she smiled again.

'Yes, I do want to do it. So much.'

Pointer heard the confidence in her voice and saw conviction in her eyes. He smiled. '*I knew I could trust you, Elena, just like you've grown to trust me. So we're going to change things slightly from now on. Sometimes I'll speak to you like this, and then you reply just like you are now. But sometimes I'll send a message like we've been doing all along. And I'll tell you whether or not to send a message back through the BlackBerry. OK?*'

Elena nodded. 'Yes. But why?'

Pointer's voice was calm and reassuring. '*Just a little extra security. We don't want anything to go wrong now we're so close.*'

'No, said Elena, staring at the screen as though

she was looking into his eyes. 'No, we don't.'

'*Good. So this is what you need to do next . . .*'

* * *

In the Four Seasons Fergus was becoming increasingly anxious as no further messages appeared on the Xda.

Like Deveraux, he liked to be in control—if not of the operation, then at least of his own part in it. But his role now was unclear; he'd flown across the Atlantic to help Elena and now he was doing nothing. Elena's life was in danger and he was sitting on his arse waiting for something to happen. That wasn't Fergus Watts; the time had come to push Deveraux into pulling Elena out.

'Look, Marcie,' he said loudly, causing Deveraux to turn and face him. 'You killed Joey; I understand that. In your position I would probably have done the same thing. But this isn't necessary. We'll get Black Star now; you said so yourself. Don't be responsible for the deaths of father *and* daughter. Get Elena out of there now.'

* * *

Back in The Hamptons, Pointer was about to click on the link on his computer that allowed him to speak to Elena. But he stopped and stared at Fergus and Deveraux. 'So, you *know* Elena.' His eyes focused on Deveraux. 'And you killed her father. How interesting. How very interesting.' His piercing eyes turned to Elena again. 'And you, my special Angel,' he whispered, 'you are part of it all. How much do *you* know?'

192

38

Marcie Deveraux's Xda rang. She turned to look through the picture window at the Manhattan skyline as she answered the call. 'Yes, Mick?'

'We've got him this time. His name is Pointer, Charles Pointer, and he's in The Hamptons. We're on the way.'

'So you managed to trace him through Ramirez's mobile phone.'

'Yeah.'

'Good. What do we know about Pointer?'

'Millionaire. Computer genius. Sold up his business five years ago. It's all being e-mailed to you.'

Deveraux could hear the screaming engine of Fran and Mick's hire car. She stared out of the window as Mick quickly gave her more details of what had happened at the East 96th Street penthouse.

'How long will it take you to get to Pointer?' she said when Mick had finished.

'The speed Fran's driving, ninety minutes max.'

'Good. Call me before you go sterile.'

Deveraux ended the call and turned round to bring Fergus up to speed. But Fergus wasn't there. She ran to the bathroom and threw open the door. No Fergus.

He was nowhere in the penthouse. He had gone. Deveraux rushed back into the sitting room and was relieved to see the sheet of paper the consulate technician had left for her on the table. He had written down the number of Fergus's new mobile phone.

Deveraux snatched the paper from the tabletop and grabbed her Xda. She punched in the unfamiliar number.

*   *   *

Fergus was already outside the Four Seasons, being shown into a cab by a uniformed porter.

'Roosevelt Hotel first,' he said to the driver. 'And I need you to wait a couple of minutes and then take me on to the Hotel Pennsylvania. Quick as you can.'

His new mobile phone was ringing in his pocket. Deveraux's number. He killed the call. It rang again. Deveraux. He ignored it. He would have turned the phone off completely but he needed to keep it on in case Danny called.

As the taxi worked its way through the traffic, Fergus ran through possible options for when he got to the Pennsylvania.

His phone beeped. A text message from Deveraux.

GOT BS. CALL ME.

Fergus punched the shortcut for Deveraux's number.

'How dare you walk out on me!' she bawled. 'I ordered you to stay here!'

'I'm just doing what I came here to do,' said Fergus. 'I'll look after Elena while you deal with Black Star.'

'That's exactly what I have done! His name is Charles Pointer; he's holed up in The Hamptons.

194

This will all be over in less than two hours.'

'So we pull Elena out now. I'll warn Danny I'm on my way and make the mix safe as soon as I get there.'

'No, Watts, you will not. Elena stays there, keeping Black Star company until Fran and Mick take him down. If you pull her out now, you will almost certainly be responsible for losing us Black Star and setting him free to kill again. Do *not* pull her out!'

*　　　*　　　*

Charles Pointer had heard only one side of the telephone conversations. But it was enough.

Herman was dead—he must be if they had his cell phone. His loyal servant, his only friend, the one person in the world who had understood and shared his grief at the loss of Chuck. He was gone. They had both known, without ever saying, that it would end this way for them. They had silently accepted it, and in one way Pointer was envious of Herman. It was over now for him. He was at peace.

Pointer realized then that what he too desired more than anything was peace. But his ultimate act of revenge had to be carried out. He would make certain that it happened, even if he was not alive to see it.

He had less than two hours. He would not run; he would not try to escape; it was probably impossible now, and besides, he no longer wanted to escape.

His mind was working quickly. It was obvious that he had been set up. He thought back to the way he had first encountered Elena as she sought help on the Deep Web. He had helped her hack into first the MI5 computer system and then the British government's Permanent Joint Headquarters mainframe computer at Northwood. She had been desperate to access top-secret information in the SECRET: ULTRA files stored on the mainframe.

Those exploits had been for real; Pointer had no doubt about that.

Quickly he ran through the sequence of events. Elena had been searching for information to clear her friend's grandfather of accusations of treachery.

The exploit had been a success; Elena had confirmed that when she made contact again on the Deep Web.

But what had happened in the interim?

Pointer smiled an ironic smile. He looked at the video picture of Marcie with admiration as he realized that, had he had more time, he would probably have rejected Elena as an Angel.

But he hadn't. He'd made a mistake, and even geniuses made mistakes.

It was all so clear now: Elena had been recruited by the very people she had battled against.

Send a hacker to catch a hacker. Clever, very clever.

And yet, perhaps not clever enough.

His eyes flicked to the picture of Elena as she worked on in the hotel room. His mistake was going to prove fatal for him, but not for his mission.

He was confident that Elena was his now. Not theirs. He knew he had turned her completely. His enemies had made their mistake by offering him up such a vulnerable target. This was no seasoned intelligence operative; this was an inexperienced teenager, full of doubts and conflicts, suffering from huge emotional pain after her father's disappearance. And he still had that card to play.

Could she even now be playing a double game? He watched her for a few minutes more. Elena was risking her life by just making the device, and she was doing it with total commitment, in exactly the same way as his other Angels had.

No. He pushed the doubt from his mind. Elena would carry out his mission. The watchers would not stop her, not now.

39

Fergus was finding the walk down the concrete fire escape stairs at the Pennsylvania difficult and painful. He had taken the elevator to the floor above Elena's and was making his way down to RV with Danny.

Danny was relieved and delighted to see his grandfather; suddenly it seemed far more possible that they would all get out of this alive.

But Fergus had no time for greetings. 'Is she still coming out to get ice?'

'Every fifteen minutes or so.'

Fergus pulled the clear plastic bag of dull white powder from his pocket and Danny's eyes widened as he saw it.

'Is that . . . ?'

Fergus nodded. 'Yeah, cocaine. Makes the PE inert. Something good coming from this shit, eh? I picked up this little trick in Colombia. I was buying it in Oxford, a bit at a time. There's other stuff that'll do the same job, but this is the easiest to get hold of. I hope she can use it.' He stared through the small window. 'Which one's her room?'

'Fifth door down to the left; right-hand side. The ice machine is on our side, about halfway towards her door.'

They were suddenly aware of voices and they quickly ducked down below the window as a group of German tourists passed the fire escape door and headed on, past Elena's room towards the lifts.

'The next time Elena comes out, I'll—' Fergus stopped mid-sentence as he stood up and looked through the window. Elena's door was opening. 'Stay here.'

As Elena closed the door behind her, a large paper cup in each hand, she looked up and saw Fergus emerge from the door to the fire escape. She smiled briefly, and then Fergus was glad to see that she remembered her training and ignored him completely. He limped slowly towards her with the bag of white powder tucked under his jacket.

As they got closer, he heard the ping of the elevator as it stopped at the eighth floor. It was round the corner, past Elena's room, but already he could hear the sound of people approaching.

Fergus ignored the excited female voices. They were speaking Italian; this place was like the United Nations. The brush contact was on— nothing would stop it now; this might well be the last ice trip. Fergus fixed his eyes on Elena's and kept moving.

They were just a couple of steps away from each other when the Italian tourists turned the corner and came in their direction. Fergus dropped the bag into one of Elena's paper cups. 'Mix it,' he said as they passed each other.

He saw Elena's eyes widen, and a brief look of panic crossed her face. However, she didn't hesitate as she made her way to the vending machine room, and Fergus stood to one side as the three Italian woman nodded their thanks and continued down the corridor. Fergus didn't look back. He went straight on to the lifts and pressed the button to go up.

As the lift doors opened and Fergus stepped inside, he was praying that giving the cocaine to Elena would be enough until they could get her out. And at least now there was a chance that no one would die.

40

The explosive was made. The pale yellow, waxy mix was drying and hardening. Pointer watched as Elena removed a khaki-coloured fisherman's vest from one of the carrier bags. The vest had been her final purchase during the shopping expedition.

He'd allowed Elena to turn down the air conditioning now that the cooking was over, and the room temperature had returned to normal.

He watched carefully as she gingerly formed the semi-dry explosive into small slabs, which she gradually packed into the long rear pocket of the close-fitting vest.

Many of his instructions to Elena had been given directly to her via the TV, while others had been sent over on the website. Pointer wanted to keep

Marcie exactly where she was while Elena completed the IED preparation.

Much of what he sent over only hinted at what Elena was doing, leaving Marcie to assume that additional instructions had been sent previously.

He would then speak directly to Elena through the television in her room, but Marcie, in her suite at the Four Seasons, heard nothing of that.

*　　　*　　　*

Fergus and Danny were behind the fire escape door, keeping a trigger through the small window. Each time a hotel guest passed they would duck down out of sight, grateful that no one, so far, had decided they wanted the exercise of a walk down the stairs.

Fergus had given Danny a quick briefing on what had happened following his arrest at Heathrow, and Danny was growing more anxious by the minute. He checked his watch and then looked at Fergus. 'Not long now, surely.'

Fergus was on stag, staring through the window towards Elena's room. 'Soon as we hear from Deveraux, we get Elena out of that room. I'll make the device safe and you take her away from here. We'll RV at the entrance to Madison Square Garden, over the road. Then it's out of the city and out of Deveraux's way.' He gently kicked Danny with his good leg. 'Your turn on stag.'

As Danny took over at the window, Fergus slid down the wall and gingerly stretched out his injured leg.

He pulled out his mobile phone and started dialling Deveraux's number. 'What's happening?'

he asked as soon as she answered. 'Have they dropped him yet? The IED has got to be made safe and the room made sterile. I need to know what's going on!'

'You will,' hissed Deveraux. 'They know exactly what they're doing!

'But it's taking too long! She hasn't been out for more ice, which means she's making the PE. She could leave for the target at any moment. I need to know the minute it's safe to get her out of there!'

'Then get off the phone and wait for my call!' yelled Deveraux. She cut the call dead.

Danny moved away from the window as an elderly British couple approached along the corridor and walked slowly past, muttering to each other about the confusing American purchase tax they seemed to be paying on everything they bought.

Danny had been listening to Fergus's call. 'Elena is safe with the cocaine in the mix, right?'

'If she's managed to add it, yes. But Deveraux's a problem too. I want us out of her reach the second Black Star is dropped. I don't care about making the room sterile; Deveraux can do that. All I'm interested in is keeping the three of us alive.' He looked at Danny. 'You know how Deveraux likes to clean house.'

41

Fran and Mick were about ten miles from their destination. They had made their plans and knew full well they had no time to refine an intricate

201

scheme to take down Black Star. They would carry out what was known as an Emergency Response, which comprised the three elements of the Fergus Watts version of SAS: Speed, Aggression and Surprise.

They had long ago left the towering skyline of Manhattan behind them and kept to the fast lane of Highway 495, heading east towards Long Island, land of the rich and famous.

Their headlights illuminated the exit highway signs displaying a strange mix of locations: names like Patchogue and Lake Ronkonkoma from the rich Native American past mingled with others such as Smithtown and Kings Park, which had been bequeathed to the area by the first English settlers.

Fran and Mick were again wearing two pairs of surgical rubber gloves, just as they had when they broke into the Winnebagos, and for the attack on the East 96th Street apartment. As before, they had to ensure that they left no identifying traces during the operation.

Mick was checking Fran's P11 as the hire car's headlights pierced the darkening evening. He made sure the barrel was firmly connected into the pistol grip as he wiped it clean of any prints. He pressed the small tester button on the back of the grip: a small pinprick of red light appeared in the centre of the button to show that the battery still had power and the chunky five-round barrel was still in place.

Once he was satisfied that the weapon was fully functional, he began to check his own P11.

'We know yours works,' said Fran with a smile.

Mick looked at the empty barrel, the one that had taken down Herman Ramirez. 'Yeah, it works fine.'

They were both carrying an extra barrel in their pockets, giving Fran ten rounds, Mick nine. They worked on the theory that if they needed more than that, they weren't doing their job properly, or were so deep in the shit that even another hundred rounds wouldn't help them.

Mick picked up the road map that was resting on his knees. 'Nearly there,' he said. 'Three more exits.'

*   *   *

Pointer knew the hunters were closing in fast. He sent another message to Elena.

Open the padded envelope now, Gola. U no wots inside. U no wot 2 do with it.

Before Elena could punch out her reply, Pointer spoke to her directly. *'I know you don't know what to do with what's inside the envelope, Elena, but that message is for the person watching us.'*

He saw Elena's eyes widen and her breath come more quickly. She knew.

'Who's watching?'

There was a slight pause before Pointer replied. *'The woman who sent you here to find me, Elena.'*

'You . . . you know about her?' Elena's voice was breathy with panic.

'Of course I know about her—and everyone else too. I'm curious. Why didn't you tell me about Marcie?'

He saw Elena looking desperately around the room as if searching for an answer.

'*Elena,*' Pointer demanded again. '*Why didn't you tell me? Are you working for them?*'

Elena came close to the TV. She spoke urgently into the speaker.

'I was—once—at the beginning. But I'm not now. I promise. They're just using me, and I decided to let them . . . I want to do this thing. Nothing else matters to me now. My dad's gone, my friends—' Her voice broke. 'My only friend doesn't care any more, he just wants to be a soldier like his granddad.'

Pointer didn't say anything. Could this be an act? He saw tears running down Elena's face.

'Black Star?' she said, the note of desperation rising in her voice. 'Don't leave me! I want to be an Angel!'

That was enough. Pointer was convinced.

'*Don't worry, Elena,*' he said. '*You're still my Angel. My very special Angel.*'

'Thank you!'

He could hear the relief in her voice and saw the smile as she wiped away her tears.

'*They've lost their battle, Elena. They never really cared for you, just as you said. All they care about is catching me. Marcie is at the Four Seasons Hotel, watching our messages. They know what you are doing and how dangerous it is. But do they do anything about it? No.*'

Elena slumped and nodded. 'I know,' she said wearily. 'But I don't really care. It's not important now. What do we do next?'

Pointer smiled. He was right. He knew he was right.

'*We're gonna do something great tonight. Now find the padded envelope I sent you.*'

Elena reached for the envelope. Inside were a small square battery, a wooden clothes peg, some fishing line and a small sliver of plastic. The piece of plastic had a tiny hole close to one edge, and one end of the fishing line had been threaded through and tied securely.

'*There are two drawing pins at the bottom,*' Pointer told her. '*Make sure you get those, and the invitation.*'

Elena delved deeper into the envelope and took out the drawing pins and a printed invitation card.

She read the words on the stylish embossed card and turned back to the TV. 'Is that where I'm going?'

'*Yes,*' said Pointer. '*It'll be a grand occasion and I only wish I could be there with you. But tonight it all ends for me too, Elena. I shall be making the ultimate sacrifice as well. After you, I promise. I told you before that when the time was right I would do it. It's only right that we both go tonight.*'

Elena nodded and smiled. 'I'm glad.'

She placed the invitation on the bed and looked at the bizarre assortment of items she had pulled from the envelope. 'So what do I do now?'

42

Fran and Mick had found Pointer's imposing, Gothic-style mansion in The Hamptons.

As they did a drive past, their car headlights picked out the two-metre-high chain-link fence surrounding the house and gardens. The fence would be no barrier to them.

The house stood well back in the grounds, and as they drove by, it appeared to be in total darkness. But then, when they were almost past, Mick looked back and saw the slightest chink of light coming from a ground-floor room on the east side of the building.

'He's in there,' he said as the vehicle moved on. 'Looks just the place for a recluse.'

A little more than half a mile further along the road, they came to a small shopping parade and Fran parked up close to a Food Lion supermarket. Nearby was a Blockbuster and a scattering of gift shops and galleries packed with souvenirs and scenic watercolours for weekend visitors to the area.

Fran and Mick were in a hurry to get the job done, but that didn't mean cutting corners. SOPs still had to be followed as part of the Emergency Response.

First they both took a good look at the online photograph of Pointer they had been provided with; they had to make certain they killed the right man. The photograph was more than five years old, taken at the last shareholders meeting Pointer had attended. It was good enough.

Next they began emptying their pockets: they had to be sterile of anything that might be dropped and discovered later—there must be no traces to lead back to them, or even to the hotel where they were staying. A single fingerprint could link them to Pointer and the house, so short-term precautions had to be taken, just in case they got away with the attack but were then lifted as they tried to leave the country.

If they were killed—and that was always a

possibility—there would be no trace of them on any records; the US police would have two unidentifiable bodies, because Mick and Fran were deniable operators.

They were ready to leave the vehicle but there was one more thing to do. Fran hit the dial of her Xda and Deveraux answered immediately. 'Yes?'

'We're sterile,' said Fran, and then gave her the details of the vehicle's location. 'If we don't call within two hours, the vehicle will need a pick-up.'

It was an SOP. If neither of them made it back to the car, couriers from the British Consulate would come out to collect it.

'Change of normal procedure,' Deveraux told her. 'Take your mobile and cache it close to the target house. I need to know the second the job is done, and I need it done quickly.' She hung up.

Mick had shoved his Xda into the glove compartment of the hire car, but Fran's now had to go with them and be cached, just in case they didn't leave the house alive. In that event the Xda would remain hidden and the operation would still be deniable. They couldn't use Black Star's home phone or mobile because calls from those would eventually be traced back to Deveraux.

Mick saw Fran tucking her Xda into her jeans. 'What you doing? Bad drills, Fran.'

'She's flapping. Wants to know he's down ASAP.'

They got out of the car and went round to the boot to collect the ready bag, which Mick slung over his shoulders. It wasn't the normal type of ready bag they would carry back in the UK, which would have been task-orientated and packed by them.

This was prepacked, the ready-bag version of an

oven-ready meal. It was called Packet Oscar, a one-bag-fits-all-jobs kit. There were many other prepacks, such as Packet Tango, a trauma pack, and Packet Victor, which contained safe-cracking equipment.

They had a trek of half a mile back to the target house. P11s in one jacket pocket and spare barrel in the other, they began to run through the shopping parade and into the darkness, only slowing to a walk when car headlights approached.

The Emergency Response plan had, of necessity, to be simple. They had decided on what was known as their 'rolling start line', which would begin the moment they climbed the fence surrounding the target house.

They had no idea what, if any, security measures Black Star had in place and they had no time to find out. If they got over the fence and approached Black Star without tripping alarms or security lights, it would be a bonus. If they did trip an alarm system and lost the element of surprise, they would just push forward with speed and aggression until they reached him and took him down. There wasn't time to faff about.

They covered the half-mile quickly and walked along the high fence, looking for the best place to climb it. The house sat about two hundred metres back, surrounded by neat lawns and conifers.

They reached the end of the fence line on the western side of the house. Fran was leading the operation: she was the boss and she would make the decisions. 'We climb here.'

There was no need for further discussion—it slowed things down, and they both knew exactly what to do.

208

Quickly Fran kneeled by the base of the upright post where the fence changed direction and began to pull away the loose topsoil with both hands. She dug a small hole and then slipped her Xda into a couple of spare surgical gloves she had brought from the car. The Xda was covered and hidden within a few seconds and would be waiting for them if the mission was a success. If not, it would hopefully remain underground for many years.

Fran stood up and began to scramble up the fence. Mick had the bag handles over each shoulder, wearing it like a bergen. As Fran scrambled over the top of the fence, Mick followed her up. They hadn't seen any alarm systems on the fence—no motion detectors or cameras. But it made no real difference now; the attack was on.

43

Pointer was looking at Elena, who was dressed in her black designer suit and crisp white shirt. She looked as wonderful as he had imagined. There was absolutely no sign of the fisherman's vest packed with the PE she had made. He had calculated that it would fit perfectly beneath the three-quarter-length jacket. And it was there, ready to detonate the moment Elena tugged on the length of fishing line that dangled from her right sleeve.

It was a crude but effective device. The small cylindrical detonator was pushed into the PE, which was in the long poacher's pouch at the back of the vest. Coming from the det were two long thin steel wires; each ran to and around a terminal of the slim twelve-volt battery, which was held in one of the many small pockets at the front of the vest.

In normal circumstances this would allow the electrical current to complete the circuit, which would trigger the det. The power of that small, but still potentially deadly explosion would then instantly detonate the PE. But, under instructions from Pointer, Elena had made a break in the circuit before connecting the det wires to the battery by using the sliver of plastic, the clothes pegs and the two drawing pins.

She had cut one of the det wires, and then wrapped the end of the length coming from the det around the shaft of one of the drawing pins. The pin had then been pushed into one inner side of the clothes peg, at the end, where the two halves of the peg usually snap together to hold clothes on a washing line.

Elena had then repeated the process with the second length of cut wire, pushing the second drawing pin into the inner side of the other half of the peg. When she released the pressure on the two halves of the peg, the two drawing pins snapped together. If the two det wires were connected to the battery now, the circuit would be completed as the current passed through the two drawing-pin heads, which were touching. But Elena had prevented that. For now.

This was because of the thin blue sliver of plastic. It was about the size of a fifty-pence coin, with one end of the fishing line tied securely to it. Elena had opened the peg, slid the plastic between the two drawing pins and released the pressure on the peg. The plastic was held firmly between the two pins and would now prevent the circuit from being completed when the det wires were connected to the battery.

When Elena dressed, she had run the fishing line down the right sleeve of her jacket. Finally she had connected the two detonator wires to the battery.

She was ready. Everything was totally hidden, ready to fulfil its devastating task at a single sharp tug of the fishing line. The sliver of plastic would then be pulled free, the two pegs would meet, the circuit would be completed and the device would detonate. Instant revenge.

Pointer spoke softly to Elena. *'You look wonderful, Elena. Ready to go?'*

'Yes, I'm ready.'

'Good. Just open your jacket so I can see our device.'

Elena did as he asked. Pointer looked closely, straining his eyes to ensure the det leads were securely wrapped around the battery terminals and were running to the det. They were. Elena was a walking bomb.

'That's fine, Elena. Now do up your jacket and turn around so that I can check it doesn't show.'

Elena turned slowly in front of the blank TV screen, and as she did so, Pointer's eyes switched to the bank of small CCTV monitors on a shelf behind his computer.

Each monitor showed a light green picture from the night-viewing cameras dotted about the house and garden. The screens were covered with small see-through dots: motion detectors. If anything crossed two or more of the dots, the monitors set

211

off their alarms. The alarms had begun to sound.

'*Time to leave now, Elena. Don't forget the invitation, but leave the BlackBerry. You won't need that any more.*'

Elena picked up the invitation from the bed and held it in her left hand; she was ready to leave.

'*There's just one more thing I have to tell you,*' said Pointer softly. '*And I'm sad that you have to learn this from me rather than from the people who told you they were your friends.*'

He could see the questioning look in Elena's eyes but she said nothing.

'*They've all been keeping a terrible secret from you, Elena.*'

'Secret . . . ?'

On the CCTVs Pointer could see two shadowy figures as they reached the western side of the house, having deliberately avoided the dim light coming from the study on the eastern side.

Pointer knew he had only minutes left as he revealed the final secret. '*Your dad is dead, Elena. Marcie killed him. I heard her talking about it with Watts. They all know but they chose not to tell you.*'

For a second he almost panicked as he saw Elena's right hand clench into a fist, and he thought that she was about to explode the device. Her face was etched with pain and her legs seemed to almost give way as she sat down on the bed and stared at the blank TV screen.

Pointer spoke gently. '*They lied to you, Elena, they all lied, but I can't keep secrets from you. You deserve the truth. We've both lived with our pain; we'll both have our revenge as we die. I'll be with you through this, Elena, watching you all the way.*'

Elena's fist relaxed its tight grip on the fishing

212

line. When she spoke, her voice was deep and almost unrecognizable. 'Thank you,' she breathed.

'*Thank you?*' answered Pointer after a moment.

'For telling me. They're evil. All of them. Evil.'

'*Yes. And there's so much evil in this world, Elena. It's time to go now. If they try to stop you, if anyone tries to stop you, you must detonate the device.*'

Elena nodded. 'I will.'

'*Goodbye, Elena. Very soon we'll both be at peace.*'

Pointer watched his final Angel walk to the door and leave the room. He heard voices from the corridor; then the door closed and there was silence.

*　　　*　　　*

Outside Elena's room a large group of tourists were milling around, talking excitedly, some clutching *Phantom of the Opera* programmes. They were evidently gathering for a Broadway outing, but had just realized that two of their group had not turned up.

In the stairwell Fergus and Danny had ducked down beneath the window again to avoid being seen. Fergus cursed silently, counting the seconds, looking at his watch as he was forced to wait. He bobbed up to peer through the window, but his view was obscured by the mass of people. There was nothing he could do.

The tourists stood and chatted while the group leader went off to rouse the latecomers from their room. No one took the slightest notice of Elena, as she stepped into the corridor and started walking towards the lift.

Watching the CCTV cameras, Pointer could see the two figures checking windows and doors as they attempted to find a way into the house. Their faces were quite clear now and Pointer recognized them from the attacks on his Winnebagos.

Quickly he sent another message to Elena's BlackBerry, which was still in her room. He wanted to keep Marcie Deveraux guessing for as long as possible.

Great goin. Ur doin well!!! Need 2 wait 30 mins now. Take a rest. U need it!!!

On his computer, Pointer watched Deveraux pick up her own Xda and punch in a number. He heard her voice clearly: 'He's making her wait for thirty. You can stop flapping now, Watts; it'll all be over before then. Wait out.'

Pointer smiled as Deveraux cut the call. 'Not quite over, Marcie,' he said. He clicked a link on his computer and closed down the connection to the Xda at the Four Seasons. 'No more clues for you,' he said as he looked at the CCTV monitors and saw that the two intruders were approaching the main door at the front of the house.

He opened a drawer in his desk and pulled out an old .45 revolver, thinking again how impressive the operation to hunt him down had been. He opened the chamber to reveal six rounds. The weapon felt comfortable in his hands, even though he himself had never been a military man.

His grandfather had used it during the First World War, and his father had carried it during the

214

Second. When he returned home at the end of the war he had handed it over to his son, confidently predicting that it would never again be used in a conflict and telling him to keep it as a family memento. The Pointers were businessmen and industrialists: they would never have any use for weapons of war.

But Charles Pointer II had a use for the .45 now.

He watched as the man and the woman pushed against the top and bottom of the front door and realized they were checking to see if it was bolted from the inside.

The man took off the bag he had on his back, delved inside and pulled out a cylinder of steel about twenty centimetres in length and similar in diameter to a Coke can. From one end protruded a small shaft; from the other, two short lengths of steel, like handles.

Pointer was intrigued. The man passed the cylinder to his partner, who placed the shaft end against the large cylinder lock on the door. As she did so, the man took a metal-headed mallet from his bag and stood back with the mallet head poised.

The woman nodded and the man smashed the mallet into the end of the cylinder. Pointer heard the noise but continued to watch in fascination as his two potential assassins worked quickly and efficiently.

The man dropped to his knees, grabbed the two handles, turned the cylinder and then kicked open the door. His partner had already taken out a strange-looking pistol. As they entered the house, Pointer's scientific brain was working out that the shaft of the cylinder device must be made of titanium so that it was strong enough to smash the keyway of the lock and the pins, obliterating the key code and enabling the cylinder to be turned easily. He was impressed.

But then he turned to look at the .45. He pulled back the hammer all the way so that it clicked into position and shifted the chamber a little, lining up a round to be fired when the trigger was pulled.

He could hear the pair approaching, running down the marble floors towards his study. He turned off the lamp on his desk so that only his computer and the monitors were casting their pale blue light in the darkness.

He was ready.

He thought of Elena, making her way towards her date with death.

As the door to his study burst open and the woman ran in, weapon up, Pointer thought of Chuck, and as the moment of death approached, he suddenly felt more exhilaratingly alive than he had for five long years.

The man was immediately behind his partner, but at first neither of them spotted Pointer in the dim light. But they both saw the flicker of movement as he pushed the revolver into his mouth, pointed it upwards towards his brain and pulled the trigger. Charles Samuel Pointer II had not let assassins take his life; he had been in control of events until the very end.

*   *   *

The small room resounded to the thunderous roar of the .45 as Fran and Mick dived to the floor, taking cover and firing towards the sound of the weapon's report at the same time.

There was no further noise; the silence told the story.

Cautiously Mick got to his feet and found the switch for the room's main light.

Pointer was still sitting on his chair, his head lolling over to one side, the back of it missing. Blood was splattered on the ceiling, the walls, on the computer and the monitor screens.

As they moved towards him, Fran and Mick saw that Pointer's body had taken three further rounds from their P11s.

Fran went over to the wall behind the computer and pulled off the photograph of Elena, shoving it down into her jacket pocket as Mick checked out the body.

'He doesn't look all that much like the photo but it's definitely him.'

'Saved us a job, anyway,' said Fran as she searched through the desk and shelves for anything that might compromise the mission.

Mick pulled the PC from the desk, smashed it onto the ground and then stamped on it several times until the hard drive was exposed. Fran wrenched it out and then shouted one word: 'Kitchen!'

Her partner knew exactly what to do. In the kitchen he went directly to the cooker and ripped out the gas pipe. He heard the expected hiss of gas and cleared the room speedily, leaving the door open, and then running to other rooms to look for gas fires.

'You got two minutes!' he heard Fran yell.

Mick was closing every door where there was no gas fire, ensuring that the gas escaping from the kitchen would head directly towards Pointer's study.

At the far end of the corridor there was a huge lounge with a log-effect gas fire. He tore out the piping, heard the escaping gas and ran from the room, leaving the door open.

'All done. RV at the door!'

Fran had piled up furniture, paper and anything flammable she could lay her hands on, around, beneath and even on Pointer.

With the lighter she had grabbed from the ready bag she lit the paper and saw the flames spread over his body. With the computer's hard drive shoved into her jacket along with Elena's photograph, she hurtled down the corridor to the front door, the smell of gas making her gag.

As Fran emerged, Mick pulled the door shut and they ran back to the fence. Fran went over the top and jumped down as Mick started to climb. By the time he hit the ground, Fran had dug the Xda out of the mud, pulled it from the surgical gloves and was punching in Deveraux's number.

They started back towards the car and the night sky suddenly changed to daylight as the ground floor of the house erupted in flames.

44

Deveraux pulled the Xda away from her ear as the sound of the explosion and shattering glass drowned out what Fran was telling her. But she had heard enough to say, 'Well done. End ex.'

That was enough. She closed the call and instantly rang Fergus's mobile. 'Black Star is dead.

End ex. Get her out.'

*   *   *

Fergus nodded to Danny. The corridor was finally clear and Danny wrenched open the door and went hurtling towards Elena's room while Fergus followed, still with the phone to his ear as Deveraux told him what to do before they left the country. Fergus was going through the motions, letting Deveraux give orders he had no intention of obeying.

Danny was knocking on the door and trying the handle but was getting no response. He turned to his grandfather with a look of fear and confusion.

'Deveraux, shut up!' said Fergus into his mobile. 'Call Elena.'

'What?'

'Call the BlackBerry! She isn't opening up!' He hung up.

Danny put his ear to the door. 'Elena? Open up! End ex! Open up!'

There was still no response and they heard the sound of the BlackBerry's ring tone going unanswered.

'Maybe she's hurt,' said Danny. 'The fumes . . .'

Fergus pushed his grandson to one side. 'Give me your key card. Come on, quickly!'

He pulled the key ring with the two small torches from his pocket as Danny handed over his key card.

'Elena?' said Fergus more loudly. 'If you can hear me, open up!'

There was still no response. The BlackBerry stopped ringing.

'Get on stag,' said Fergus to Danny urgently.

219

Danny turned away from the door and watched the corridor. Fergus pulled away the DO NOT DISTURB sign and dropped to his knees, feeling a stab of pain shoot through his injured leg. He slid the key card into the slot, then switched on the UV light torch and moved it rapidly from side to side along the slot.

He was attempting to confuse the UV light that shone from the lock onto the metallic strip of the card to check the opening code.

Nothing happened. 'Shit!' He pulled the card from the slot and started again. 'Come on, come on!'

The door lock clicked open, and at the same time they heard the ping of the elevator doors.

They pushed their way into the room and closed the door. Fergus instantly recognized the acid smell. 'Elena?' he shouted.

Danny pushed open the bathroom door. 'She's not here—she's gone!'

Fergus looked in the wardrobe, hoping desperately to find the IED. When Danny emerged from the bathroom, he spotted the bag of cocaine sticking out from under the bed. It hadn't even been opened.

'Granddad, look!'

Fergus stared. 'Oh shit!'

On the bed the BlackBerry began to ring again.

'Danny, check the DLB,' said Fergus. 'Do it!'

Danny rushed to the door and headed for the DLB as Fergus tried to gather his thoughts, hoping his worst fears were unfounded. He snatched up the BlackBerry and answered the call. 'Elena?'

It was Deveraux.

'She's gone,' he told her, 'and the device has

gone with her! You said we had another thirty! We've missed her, and I don't know what's in her head. Maybe he *has* groomed her; maybe she *is* going through with it!'

Danny raced back into the room. In his hand was the invitation card that Elena had taken from the padded envelope earlier that evening.

'She's gone to the Time Warner Center, where she was last night,' he yelled as he thrust the invitation towards Fergus.

Fergus read the words on the card, still holding the phone to his ear.

MS ELENA OMOLODON

PLEASE JOIN OUR CELEBRATION IN THE TIME WARNER BUILDING IN THE MAGNIFICENT NEW TWIN TOWERS AT COLUMBUS CIRCLE

BLACK TIE
HANOVER FINANCE

As Fergus stared at the card, he heard Deveraux's voice. 'Where is she? Did Danny say the Time Warner Center? Is that it? Tell me what he said. Watts, I want—!'

Fergus cut the call. He kept his voice low as he

spoke to Danny, trying to keep him calm. 'Listen in. I don't know what's going on, Danny, but it could be all this grooming *has* affected her. She's told us where she is—maybe that's so we can find her or maybe it's—'

'—so we'll see her detonate the device?' said Danny. 'It can't be that, Granddad. It can't be! She wouldn't do that!'

'Get to Columbus Circle now—run, it'll be quicker. I'll get there as soon as I can.'

Danny was staring, listening intently as his grandfather continued.

'Do whatever it takes, but you've got to make sure the two det leads are disconnected from the battery, then you have to twist the leads together. Remember everything I told you before.'

Danny nodded and turned to go.

'Wait!' said Fergus. 'You *must* twist the leads—otherwise they become an antenna and any electricity in the air could still detonate the device. Just keep her there until I arrive. Now go!'

Danny sprinted from the room and Fergus followed. He picked up the DO NOT DISTURB card, which was lying on the floor, and hung it back on the door. Danny had already disappeared; he was tearing down the fire escape stairs.

Fergus limped towards the elevator, his leg burning with pain. Maybe he would be lucky; maybe he could pick up a cab and get to Columbus Circle quickly.

But it looked as though saving Elena was going to be down to Danny.

45

Manhattan's grid system means that it's easy to get around. The numbered streets run east to west, starting at 1st Street in Lower Manhattan to way up in the hundreds uptown, with the famous name avenues and Broadway running north to south.

In only two days, and greatly aided by his surveillance stint, Danny had quickly latched onto the system and felt he could now find his way anywhere in Manhattan without getting lost.

But getting lost wasn't the problem. Getting where he wanted to go was.

As he sprinted past shocked-looking guests and porters in the Pennsylvania reception and out through the revolving doors, he could picture his quickest route. He would simply turn to the left and head for Eighth Avenue, where he would turn right for the long run up to Columbus Circle.

It was an easy route, and Danny reckoned he could cover the distance in around twenty minutes. But as soon as he went through the doors he hit trouble.

The road was jam-packed with traffic and the pavements were heaving with New Yorkers and tourists out for a stroll, taking in the sights or window-shopping.

And no one apart from Danny appeared to be in a hurry.

He was dodging and weaving through the crowd and he didn't see the fur-coated middle-aged woman and her jacketed Pekinese until he had tripped over the dog's lead.

The Pekinese yelped, the woman yelled, and Danny went stumbling into a mobile pretzel stall trundling towards him from the opposite direction.

'Hey, buddy, watch it, will yer!' shouted the pretzel seller as Danny struggled to keep his feet.

'Sorry, sorry,' said Danny. The woman glared at him and bent down to comfort her quivering pet.

Danny started off again, until he came to the next junction and the sign with the bright red stationary figure.

He had to stop; other pedestrians were six-deep in front of him, all of them waiting for the signal to begin the cavalry-charge to the other side. Danny tried to edge his way through to the front, but he was still three back when the lights changed and everyone moved together.

It didn't get any better as he turned onto Eighth Avenue. Danny had always been a runner, but he barely managed more than five or six strides at a time before having to skid to a halt or dodge away from an oncoming pedestrian.

He was getting more and more angry and frustrated, and when he was held at another junction, he took the gamble of crossing against the lights. A car horn blared and Danny leaped back, almost into the path of a pedal taxi.

'Jerk!' yelled the rider as he swerved by. 'You got a death wish or something?'

The words just made Danny think of Elena. A death wish: was that what she had now?

*   *   *

Deveraux was pacing up and down in her room. Fergus and Danny were not answering her calls.

224

She had to consider her options and make a decision. Fran and Mick were still too far away from the city to be of any practical use. She thought about calling the New York police or even her opposite numbers in the US Security Services, but swiftly pushed the thought from her head.

Too many problems; too much explanation. She had her promotion—no, her entire future—to think of, and the only way that could be guaranteed was if *she* ensured the mission was a complete success.

Killing Black Star had been the aim of the mission—at whatever cost—and Deveraux had calculated that the cost could have been one or more of her team.

But now the cost could be numerous innocent victims, and that would be the end of all her plans. Despite Dr Jacobson's and Dudley's warnings, Deveraux had never believed that Elena really *would* go through with a suicide bombing. Now it seemed she was wrong.

There was only one option: she had to sort this herself. She had to stop Elena from detonating the device. She took the spare P11 pistol grip out of the room safe and pushed home a new barrel.

*   *   *

Fergus was almost ready to give up on his cab and drag himself up to Columbus Circle. The driver had happily headed into a traffic jam soon after Fergus got into the vehicle. When Fergus shouted at him, he eventually found somewhere to turn round and then cruised straight into a fresh snarl-up on the edge of Times Square.

'I don't understand it,' he said to Fergus with a shrug. 'It ain't usually like this. Must be something special going down tonight.' He turned round and gave a toothy grin. 'Maybe Brad Pitt is in town for a premiere. Or Nicole. She's one hot babe, that Nicole, huh?'

Fergus didn't reply, just reached into his jacket pocket for some notes and thrust them at the driver through the opening in the dividing screen. 'I'll walk.'

The driver shrugged again as Fergus threw open the door, got out of the cab and limped away up Broadway.

The Broadway theatres were ablaze with lights and illuminated posters and photographs of the latest smash hit shows.

Fergus saw none of them. He was totally focused on reaching Columbus Circle, ignoring the pain in his leg. It was as though it wasn't there. As he limped on towards his destination, he told himself it was nothing compared to some of the forced marches he had endured over the years.

All he cared about was getting to Elena. And Danny.

46

Danny saw the laser lights dancing over the Time Warner Center towers long before he reached Columbus Circle.

He was sprinting along Eighth Avenue. He still had to pause and sometimes stop completely at the crossroads, but he took stupid, crazy risks as he dodged pedestrians and vehicles.

He had to reach Elena. That was all that mattered.

He emerged into the sprawl of Columbus Circle, gasping for breath. Chauffeur-driven stretch limos and a variety of expensive, gleaming cars were starting to deposit their passengers for the big event. Dozens of camera flashes added to the light show as smiling guests walked up the red carpet.

Danny ran past them all and into the entrance of the building. There was a sign saying where the Hanover event was taking place, so he ran straight to the elevators.

Two huge guys in tuxedos stood on guard. 'Whoa there, son,' said the taller one as Danny almost skidded to a standstill. 'And where do you think you're going?'

'To . . . to the Hanover opening,' gasped Danny.

The two musclemen weren't in the mood for a smart guy. 'Invitation only, son. No one gets in without an invitation.'

Danny was struggling for breath. 'But . . . but I've *got* an invitation,' he said, reaching into a pocket and pulling out the embossed card. 'Look.'

They looked, and then they glanced at each other before the second man spoke. 'And didn't you read what it says on there about the dress code?'

Danny stared down at his trainers, jeans and bomber jacket. It wasn't what was required but he had to say something—anything. 'I didn't have time to change.'

The taller guard took a closer look at the invitation. 'What kinda dress were you planning on wearing tonight, *Ms* Elena Omolo— whatever?'

For a moment Danny considered attempting to continue with his pathetic bluff, but he knew it was useless. And another thought had come into his mind. 'Did you say that no one can get in without an invitation?'

The big guy nodded. 'That's right. No invitation, no go.'

'But my . . . my friend is meant to be there.' He held up the card. 'The invitation is hers. She left it in the hotel. I was hoping to . . . to give it to her.'

Both guards visibly relaxed. 'Why didn't you say that in the first place, instead of trying to fool us like you did?'

'I . . . I dunno. I just want to make sure she gets in.'

'Yeah,' said the guard. 'Look, you leave the invitation with me and I'll make sure she gets it when she turns up. As long as she's got some ID, that is.'

He reached out to take the invitation but Danny was already slipping it back into his pocket. 'No. No, it's all right, thanks. I'll wait for her outside. I need to see her anyway.'

'Suit yourself,' said the big guy with a shrug.

Danny was about to turn away but then he stopped. 'You're certain she couldn't have gone up there?'

'I told you,' said the guard. 'If she ain't got no invitation, she ain't at the party.'

47

Danny walked away from the Time Warner building, wondering if perhaps he'd got it all wrong: maybe Elena had left the invitation stuck to the DLB to confuse him; to send him on a wild goose chase while she carried her deadly cargo to some other venue in Manhattan.

But why? To get him out of the way? To make sure he was safe as she killed herself when the device was detonated?

He had no idea what to do next as he edged his way through a large group of new arrivals and made for Columbus Circle.

And then he saw her. Elena was standing across the road, close to the wall surrounding Central Park. She was staring directly at him.

Danny couldn't stop himself from shouting. 'Elena!'

Elena just kept staring and Danny started across the road. A car horn blared its warning and he jumped back onto the pavement.

When he looked across the road again, she had disappeared. 'Elena!' he breathed.

He pulled out his mobile and dialled. 'Granddad, I've found her.'

He explained exactly where he'd seen Elena standing, hearing the traffic and voices and Fergus's laboured breathing in the background as he talked.

'I'll be there in ten,' said Fergus. 'Be *careful*, Danny, and remember, get that det off the battery and twist the leads together. Get the IED off her and walk away. I'll do the rest. Good luck.'

Danny slipped the mobile back into his pocket, looked across the road and saw Elena again. She had moved further back into the shadows, but she was there, and she was still looking at him. Danny remembered the area well; it was almost exactly where he had been standing when he was pulled into the darkness of the park by Mick.

Danny waited for the traffic to pass. He crossed the road, walking rather than running, realizing that he needed to approach Elena with caution—the utmost caution.

He took three further steps across the wide pavement and then Elena spoke. 'Don't come any closer, Danny.'

Her voice was strange—deep and distant—and as Danny stopped moving, she looked down at her right hand, which was holding the fishing line, and raised it slightly. 'Go away, Danny, you're in danger if you stay.'

'Elena, please!' said Danny softly but urgently, knowing that he had to try to appear calm, even though his heart was pounding.

Slowly Elena lowered her hand until it rested at her side.

'Don't do it, Elena. Please? You can't do what Black Star wanted now; you won't get in. I'm not gonna give you the invitation. And Black Star's dead.'

The relief on Elena's face was obvious. She smiled. 'Is he? Oh, Danny . . . He said he was going to die, but I didn't know whether he meant it.'

Danny had no idea what she was talking about.

Elena leaned back against the wall, her hand letting go of the line. 'Why did it all take so long? I didn't know what to do and I thought he was following me, watching me, all the time. That's why I left the invitation, so you'd know where I'd gone. With this stuff on my back, I knew I didn't have long.'

Danny moved slowly towards Elena, listening to every word she said.

'I knew I wouldn't get in without the invitation and I knew I couldn't bluff Black Star and tell him that I'd tried to detonate but the mix didn't work. I came over here to get out of the way of all those people.'

'You . . . you mean, you *weren't* going to detonate the device?'

Elena stared at him. '*What?*'

'I thought . . . we thought . . .'

'I didn't know what was happening—I had to keep going—I had to carry on with the job until I knew Black Star was dead.'

'But the cocaine was still in the room. We thought you were gonna do it for real.'

'What! Why would you think that?' She paused. '*Cocaine!* Is that what . . .? I couldn't put it in the mix. He was watching me all the time! There was nowhere I could do it without him seeing.' She shuddered. 'You have no idea how awful it was! I was scared, Danny, really scared. I wanted to walk out and leave someone else to do it. But I knew I couldn't.' The words tumbled out of her.

'You're sure he's dead?' she asked again.

Danny nodded. 'Dead. Really dead.'

'You know, Danny, there were times when I lost it, lost sight of what I was doing,' she whispered. 'His voice. It took hold of me. It was so creepy. And I was playing the part so hard . . .' She took a

231

deep breath. 'You're gonna think I'm crazy, but Danny, there were moments when I . . . I started to believe . . . I thought I was going to go through with it. And then I thought of you, my dad—' Her voice broke.

'You love this stuff, Danny I don't. I hate it. The lies. The secrets.' She sighed. 'I've gotta get out. There's something I've got to do first and then I just want to go home.'

She looked down at the fishing line dangling from the jacket sleeve. 'I have to get this thing off me. We'd better go somewhere out of sight.' She started working at the buttons of the jacket. 'I couldn't take it off before. People would have seen me. I disconnected the det leads in the lift. That was all I had time for.'

'It's still dangerous,' said Danny.

'I know,' Elena replied. 'Let's go.'

As she moved slowly down the ramp leading into the park, Danny followed and took out his mobile.

'Who are you calling?' asked Elena.

'My granddad. He needs to know what's happening.'

'Not yet, Danny. I want to talk to you alone first.' She'd unbuttoned her jacket, but then she stopped. 'There's something I need to know.'

She looked closely at Danny. The lights of the city seemed far off. He could hear the traffic but it could have been a million miles away.

'Deveraux killed my dad,' she said.

'*What?*'

'It's true. Black Star told me he heard Fergus and Deveraux talking about it. Did you know? I want the truth, Danny—don't lie to me. There've been enough lies.'

Danny was still trying to get his head around what Elena had said. 'Maybe Black—'

'Did you *know*?'

'No, I didn't. Maybe Black Star just said that . . . to get you to do the bombing. How could he know?'

'He *heard* them. And I know he was telling the truth. You know what Deveraux's like. She did it. I know she did.' Elena's voice was deep with urgency. 'Danny. Did you know?'

'I promise you I didn't know,' he said.

Elena said nothing. Just stared at him, as if looking for the truth in his face.

'I've never lied to you, Elena,' he said more emphatically. 'If it is true, we'll find out. But can we get the IED off you? I've gotta call Granddad to tell him that we're in the park. He knows how to make it safe.'

They were at the bottom of the ramp, and Elena moved even further into the gloom. 'I believe you. I'm glad. But I'm still doing it.' She stared towards the lights bouncing off the Time Warner building and up into the sky.

'Doing what? I don't understand, Elena.'

She turned back to Danny as a single tear rolled down her face. 'Somehow, and I don't know how, I'm gonna kill Deveraux.'

Behind the tears in Elena's eyes was a hard look of determination that frightened Danny.

'Elena,' he said softly. 'I . . . I promised I'd always be here for you. I haven't done as good as I could have . . . I . . . I got too caught up in all this . . . stuff. Black Star. Working for . . .' He was going to say Deveraux but he knew it was the one word he had to avoid. 'Working on this mission. It made

233

me feel important. Special.'

He edged forward as he continued to speak softly. 'But I've realized it's not important,' he went on. 'None of it. Not if I haven't got you. You're the most important thing in the world to me, Elena. Honest, I swear it. More important than my granddad. More than anything.'

He swallowed hard. 'I love you, Elena. You know that. But killing someone in revenge . . . you can't kill Deveraux, you know that. It won't bring your dad back.'

Elena's body shook as she sucked in a deep, sobbing, faltering breath and tears sprang to her eyes again. She opened her mouth to speak, but no words came.

'And your dad wouldn't want it,' said Danny, fighting back his own tears. 'He'd want you to be happy, like he was. Your dad was always smiling, and laughing. That's how he'd want to see you. Always.' He paused for a moment.

'My granddad's going to get us out of here. We'll be safe and we can think things through.'

The hard look was back on Elena's face.

'Fergus knew,' she said accusingly.

'I don't think he did,' said Danny. 'He didn't tell me—' He stopped again. There were lots of things Fergus didn't tell him.

The night was still. They were only a few metres inside Central Park, but it was enough to give the illusion of woodland. The only reminder that they were in the heart of the city was the constant drone of the traffic spinning around Columbus Circle before heading off to every part of Manhattan.

Neither of them moved, but Danny was acutely conscious of the danger they were in.

Then Elena lifted her head and looked at him. He could see her shoulders relax. She smiled. It wasn't the challenging, confident smile of old, but it was a smile. A beginning.

She nodded. 'You're right. But I hate her and I'm still going to get her,' she said grimly. 'Maybe not kill her, but I'm going to get her somehow.'

Danny took a single step forward. He had to twist the det wires—make sure they were really safe. 'We'll do it together, Elena.'

And then, before he could take another step or say another word, there was a dull thud and Elena was hurled backwards with shattering force and went crashing to the ground at the base of a tree.

Danny's mouth gaped open. He tasted the blood, Elena's blood, as it ran down his face and over his lips into his mouth.

For a moment his brain was telling him that the device had detonated and killed Elena. Just Elena. But that couldn't have happened. It couldn't. It couldn't.

Then he heard Deveraux's voice: 'Move away from the device! Move away!'

Danny's head turned slowly. Nothing else would move.

Deveraux was behind him, a little to one side, her P11 still up in the firing position and pointed at Danny's head. 'Move away from the device,' she said again, her words slow and controlled. 'If you do not move, I'll take you down too. Move away. *Now.*'

Somehow Danny forced himself to take two or three shuffling steps away from Elena's body, which was lying face down and perfectly still.

'Give me your mobile phone!' said Deveraux.

'Now!'

Danny reached into his pocket and handed it over. With her pistol still in her right hand, Deveraux punched in Fergus's number, knowing he would take a call from his grandson. He did.

'Danny, I'm at the Circle. Where are you?'

'It's over,' said Deveraux. 'I need you to make the device safe.'

48

Fergus had had two minutes to prepare himself for what he saw as he walked down the ramp into the park.

But it made no difference. He was crying.

Danny was sitting against the inner wall, his head bowed over his raised knees. He didn't look up when Fergus glanced towards him before going over to Elena's body.

Deveraux was by the ramp, her weapon still in her hand. She was watching and waiting in case anyone should wander into the park.

Fergus knelt at Elena's side. Blood was still flowing from the head wound and he was relieved that he didn't have to look at her face. He couldn't have looked at her face.

He wiped the tears from his cheeks and then, slowly and expertly, he began to search for the detonator.

On the ground next to Elena's head he saw the pouch containing her passport attached to a chain around her neck. She had followed all Danny's orders.

Danny hadn't moved since Deveraux had ordered him to sit by the wall, but he looked up and saw his grandfather by Elena's body. 'She'd already disconnected the det.'

It took a long, tense sixty seconds to establish that what Danny had said was correct. Fergus nodded towards Deveraux, who took out her Xda and punched in a number. Then he got up and went over to his grandson.

Deveraux was talking into her Xda: 'Cancel the end ex. I have another job for you right now. I want you and Fran to come and clear up at Columbus Circle. Across from the Time Warner building; just inside the park. We need to dispose of a body.'

Danny's head snapped round towards Deveraux. His eyes blazed with fury but his words hissed through clenched teeth. 'It's not a body,' he snarled. 'It's *Elena!*'

Fergus rested one hand on his shoulder. 'Danny,' he said gently. Danny was still glaring at Deveraux. 'Danny,' said Fergus again.

Slowly Danny turned and looked up at his grandfather. There were no tears, not yet. All that registered on his ashen face was pain, and stunned disbelief. 'She wasn't gonna do it, Granddad,' he said. 'She wasn't gonna do it.'

Fergus carefully pulled Danny to his feet. 'Come on, we're—'

'Stand still!' Deveraux's finger was still on the P11's electronic trigger.

Fergus gripped Danny's hand tightly. 'What you gonna do, Marcie? Drop us both?' He shook his head. 'You can't do that. Know why?'

The P11 was pointed at Fergus's head but he continued without waiting for a reply.

'You'd have three bodies to clean up. That's not possible for you and your two mates. One, you might just get away with. But three? No chance. You'll be seen, and then what do you do, Marcie?'

He began to move backwards, still gripping Danny's hand. 'And there's another reason you can't pull that trigger. I have all your Oxford sit reps. We go down and they go straight to the FBI. I've still got a few friends back home, Marcie. They don't hear from me, the sit reps go to the FBI.'

He could see Deveraux's hesitation. Slowly she lowered the pistol, as Fergus pulled his grandson into the darkness of the park.

Some time later . . .

They were living in a small rented cabin on the edge of one of the Great Lakes of Canada. But they were also living a lie.

Fergus was an accomplished liar; it had long been part of his life and part of his trade. Operating covertly in the Regiment and afterwards as a K, he had found that his life had often depended upon his ability to tell completely believable lies.

He had taken on many new identities; they were all fabrications, lies. He had become so good at lying that even when challenged in a life-threatening situation, he almost believed the untruth he was telling.

That ability had spilled over into his personal life. As a young man, he had lied to his wife during their brief marriage. Sometimes it was just easier to tell a lie, as long as he remembered that lie when the time came to tell the next lie. He had lied to his son. He had lied to mates; sometimes it was necessary for their safety as well as his own. And now he had lied to his grandson.

It had always been easy for Fergus to lie because, until very recently, he had never cared enough about anyone for it to bother him too much. But now it did.

They had made their escape, heading north through Central Park, and they didn't stop travelling until they reached Canada. At first Danny was too deeply shocked to even speak. He just allowed himself to be led like a small child by his grandfather. Neither of them mentioned Elena's name.

Fergus rented the cabin and made sure they were secure, and then he contacted Deveraux; he had to—they needed money. He reminded her that if anything happened to himself or Danny, the FBI would get every one of the sit reps he had downloaded from her laptop. A few days later the cash was transferred into the bank account that Fergus had set up.

It should have been a new beginning, but it wasn't.

Spring had moved well into summer, and most days were warm and bright. But now the weather had turned; it was raining and the sky was leaden and heavy.

Danny sat against a tree trunk, getting little shelter from the rain. He reached into his jacket and took out the alias passport Fergus had got for Elena. He always kept it with him. Her name would have been Elena Higgs, according to the passport. But names didn't mean a thing. He opened the back page and looked at her photograph, and then he let his head tilt upwards against the tree trunk so that the raindrops could mingle with the tears running down his face.

When he got back to the cabin, Fergus was brewing coffee on the stove. He put two mugs and the coffee pot on the wooden table and then sat in the chair opposite his grandson.

'We need to talk, Danny.'

Danny looked hard into his grandfather's eyes. 'Do we?'

'It's about . . . the future. What we do. We can't stay here for much longer and the money we've got won't last for ever.'

The rage that had been building inside Danny

suddenly exploded like a bursting dam. 'The future! How can we talk about the future when we've never talked about the past?'

Fergus looked bewildered. 'What?'

'Why didn't you tell me Deveraux killed Joey? You owed it to me, and you owed it to Elena.'

It was out in the open. At last.

'I . . . I didn't know until near the end. It was too late to do anything about it then and it didn't make any difference as far as the—'

'As far as the mission was concerned!' yelled Danny. 'Is *that* what was most important?'

'No! Keeping you and Elena safe was what mattered most!'

'Well, you failed in that, didn't you?'

Danny grabbed one of the coffee mugs, stood up and hurled it with all his strength at the wall behind his grandfather's head. It shattered and coffee dripped down the wall.

Fergus hadn't moved a muscle. 'How did you know?' he said quietly. 'About Deveraux?'

Danny slumped back down onto his chair. 'Black Star told Elena, and Elena told me just before Deveraux killed her.'

They were silent for a few moments, both deep in their own thoughts, and then Fergus got up, fetched another mug and filled it with coffee.

'I'm sorry. When it was over, I should have told you. But I thought there was no point in you knowing now. Sometimes it's better to . . .'

'Lie?'

'To . . . to just not tell the truth.'

Danny shook his head. 'Yeah. And look where it's got us.'

'We've got to move on, Danny. Not to forget

about Elena—'

'I don't wanna talk about Elena!' said Danny, his face furious again.

'But we have to talk about the future. About what we're going to do. I can't be certain we'll be safe here. We need to work, get jobs.'

'What jobs? Another burger bar? What else could you do? And what could *I* do? All you've ever taught me is how to lie.'

He grabbed the coffee and took a gulp. 'Oh, yeah, and I also know a lot about killing now.'

Danny pushed back his chair and it scraped noisily across the floor. 'I'm going for another walk,' he snarled. 'It'll give me time to think about my career options.'

Fergus knew there was no point in arguing. They would talk more later, when Danny had calmed down. He watched his grandson go to the door, open it and step outside, leaving it open.

The cabin stood at the end of a long mud track, which rose gradually for about a hundred and fifty metres before descending again and winding on towards the town.

As Danny left the cabin, he glanced to his right. At the top of the rise in the track sat a stationary black 4x4. Danny could just hear the throb of its running engine.

'Granddad,' he said quietly, without moving back into the cabin. 'We've got company.'

THE END